THE WIDOW'S HUSBAND'S SECRET LIE

A SATIRICAL NOVELLA (NOTE: THIS MEANS IT'S ACTUALLY *SUPPOSED* TO BE FUNNY/SILLY)

FREIDA MCFADDEN

For hiunuihikhjjjkj;'/Ljk///////////////////ffgf

(Sorry, my cat walked across my keyboard so many times, I finally decided to let her write the dedication)

PROLOGUE

YOU THINK YOU KNOW WHO THE KILLER IS.

It's obvious, you say. You knew it from the first chapter. The first paragraph. The first sentence. The first *letter*.

But you are wrong. There is nothing obvious about the identity of this antagonist. I have used red herring after red herring, woven in false identities and unreliable narrators, and fabricated evidence. At least three people who you thought were dead are actually alive.

There is no possible way you could know the truth. There's no way you could ever guess that the killer is actually Steve.

Wait. Oh, crap.

Ugh. Well, nobody reads the prologue anyway.

1

I AM BROWSING SHAMPOOS AT THE DRUGSTORE WHEN I become aware that I am being followed.

I've never been followed before. Why would I? I'm not a *spy*. Yet I immediately recognize that's what's happening. It's like when you walk into a room and instinctively know that everyone was just talking about you. (That happens to me a lot.)

So that's how I know, without ever having been followed before, that there is somebody behind me, watching me. Somebody who saw me enter this drugstore and has been tracking my every move.

Before I recognized that someone was following me, I was attempting to decide which shampoo to buy. The last couple of weeks have been incredibly hard on me, and it's a comfort to get back to a mundane activity like shopping. It's my first step in returning to normal life.

My usual brand is made from tea tree oil, smells like mint, and is supposed to deep clean and refresh my scalp. But every time I shop for shampoo, I start to doubt myself. Do I need one that is more hydrating? Less hydrating? Is my hair oily or dry? How have I gotten through thirty-four years of life without knowing this basic fact about my hair?

Even without somebody watching me, it's over-whelming.

I pick up a bottle of something called coconut milk shampoo. It advertises having coconut oil and egg-white protein. I can see why I might need egg-white protein in my diet, but do I need it in my hair? I examine the bottle, studying the shockingly long list of ingredients, which includes many items that have over ten syllables, none of which are coconut or egg related.

And then, in the middle of *dodecenylsuccinate*, I whip my head around. Five seconds ago, I felt a pair of eyes boring into me. I would have bet my life on it. And now I am utterly alone in the shampoo aisle. I look left and right, but there's nobody here. Nobody is watching me.

I must be imagining it. Apparently, my life has reached a point where I am hallucinating people following me.

Shopping for shampoo should not be a stressful endeavor. I was doing this exact activity when I met Grant for the first time. I was standing in the shampoo aisle, just like today, trying to figure out if my hair needed more or less surfactant, and Grant was a few feet away, looking at the soap on the other side of the aisle.

I noticed him, of course. It was hard to ignore a man like Grant Lockwood. But the wild part was that he noticed me too.

He smiled at me with a row of startlingly perfect

teeth and said, "Whatever you are using in your hair right now, you should buy it again, because it is perfect."

Barely a year later, we were married.

I suppose it's possible that this bit of nostalgia is what brought me here in the first place. That and the fact that my shampoo bottle is nearly empty. I tried turning it upside down and shaking it as hard as I could, but I could only squeeze out a dime-sized amount of liquid.

I replace the coconut oil shampoo on the shelf and pick up my tried-and-true tea tree oil. Above all, I'm a creature of habit. Also, I want to pay for my shampoo and get the hell out of here.

I clutch the brown bottle as I walk in the direction of the cashiers. And with each step, I still can't shake that sensation of being watched. Maybe this is all in my head —a hallucination. But it *feels* like somebody is there.

I stop. Turn around again.

Still nobody.

You're losing it, Alice. Now you think you're being followed, of all things. What next?

When I'm halfway to the cash registers, I pass a display of sunglasses. In the middle of October, it's hardly sunglasses weather anymore, but I stop there anyway. The array of sunglasses is only slightly less over-whelming than the number of shampoos. I pick up a pair of dark ones that are polarized. I have no idea what that means, but it must be important because the tag on the glasses says it in big block letters.

I make a motion like I'm about to put on the pair of sunglasses, but instead, I peer into the tiny mirror meant for modeling the glasses on my face. I can clearly see my flaming-red hair, although today it looks limp and lifeless. People often compliment me on my vivid sea-green eyes, but now they are puffy, and the rims are lined with pink. I look tired.

But that's not all I see. In the mirror, I can make out a man standing behind me. Watching me. He's a few years older than me, roughly late thirties. He has dark-blond hair that is straight and laced with flecks of gold from the sun. Chiseled features. A square jaw. Determined-looking blue eyes.

I suck in a breath. This man looks *exactly* like Grant.

I watch him for as long as I dare in the reflection, and then I turn. But as expected, he has vanished, like he never existed in the first place.

I push back a wave of nausea. The resemblance between that man and Grant was uncanny. Of course, it was hard to get a good look in that sliver of a mirror, and the man was at least twenty feet away from me. It's entirely possible that I simply imagined the similarities in appearance. In fact, that is by far the best explanation.

I return the polarized sunglasses to the display. I continue marching down the aisle until I reach the cash registers and join a line that is much longer than it ought to be at two in the afternoon—there are a few people ahead of me, and they seem to be taking forever. One woman is paying with a check. A check? Really? Who pays with a check in this century? She may as well be trading with gold trinkets.

And all the while, I have a creepy-crawly sensation

in the back of my neck. I turn around one last time, searching for the man who looks like Grant. I look past the counter where you can print your photos and the snack-food aisle and the one with all the feminine hygiene products. But there's nobody there who looks like my husband.

I need to calm down. Whatever I saw in the mirror of that sunglasses display must have been my imagination. Or an optical illusion. But the important thing I need to remember is that it was *not Grant*. It was definitely not my husband standing in the middle of the drugstore and watching me while I chose shampoo and browsed sunglasses. It couldn't have been.

Because my husband has been dead for two weeks.

2

I HAVE THE MOST BEAUTIFUL HOME.

It's an old house with the first two floors fully renovated, although the attic is yet untouched. Grant owned
it for many years before I moved in, and I always
wondered why he never bothered to update the topmost
floor of the house, but I didn't probe too deeply. The
house is made of brown bricks with a white trim and a
large chimney rising majestically from the roof. The
home boasts five bedrooms that we fantasized about
filling with children after reading in a magazine that this
Long Island neighborhood had some of the best schools
in the state.

These days, it just seems empty.

When I pull into the driveway and park just outside
our two-car garage, I find a woman standing on my
front porch, wearing yoga pants and a hoodie, her
brown hair in a messy bun, clutching a large rectangular
dish. It's Poppy, my next-door neighbor and closest
friend, and she has what I presume is a casserole.

I don't want another casserole. However, ever since Grant died, it seems that people have decided that casseroles are *all* I want. I have received more of them than flowers, despite the fact that casseroles are more of a family thing, and there's just one of me. My refrigerator is only one rectangular pan away from being a solid mass of noodles and cream of mushroom soup.

I kill the engine and climb out of my Lexus, clutching the brown paper bag containing my tea tree oil shampoo. Poppy brightens when she sees me, balancing the dish on one hand so she can wave to me. For a moment, I hope that the dish will fall, spilling egg noodles and broccoli everywhere.

"Alice!" she calls out. "I brought you dinner!"

I try to smile, although I suspect the smile doesn't touch my eyes or even my nose. "That's very thoughtful."

"Just pop this in the oven for thirty minutes at 350," she chirps, even though I am well aware of how to heat up a casserole, thank you very much.

I unlock the door to the house. For a split second, I get that sensation, again, that there is somebody watching me. Poppy is smiling eagerly as she waits for me to unlock the door, but when she notices my expression, her smile falters.

"Are you okay, Alice?" she asks.

People keep asking me that. How could I be okay? My husband is dead. He was one month shy of thirty-eight years old, and he died in a fiery car wreck. How exactly am I supposed to be okay?

Yet I can't say all that. What they are really asking is

if I am going to suddenly dissolve into a blubbering mess, ripping my hair out with my fists, and then run up to the roof and throw myself off. That is the actual question.

"I'm okay," I say.

I finally manage to get the door open, and Poppy tags along after me with her casserole. "Are you hungry?" she asks. "I can heat it up for you now."

It wouldn't do to tell her that I hate casseroles with every fiber of my being. Not after she's made me five of them.

"No, thanks." I wrench open the coat closet by the front door—one of the few closets in the house that does not allow you to walk inside. I look up at the LED lights mounted on the ceiling of the closet, and I swear softly under my breath. *Useless.* "I'm not really hungry."

"I'll make you some tea, then," Poppy says.

Before I can protest that I don't actually like tea either (I find it just barely tolerable if you put a little milk in it), Poppy is inside my kitchen. She fills a pot with warm water and sets it on the stove to boil. She searches in a cupboard over the sink until she locates a box of herbal tea. It must have belonged to Grant.

While Poppy is brewing the tea, I wander into the living room. There's very little in this room that doesn't remind me of Grant. The television set is almost comically large, because he said that we have the money and should treat ourselves. There's the antique coffee table that he saw me admiring in the store and insisted on buying in spite of the outrageous price tag. Even the

Italian leather sofa still has a dent in it from where he always used to sit.

The most memories, however, are reflected in the frames sitting on the mantel over the fireplace. I step across our Oriental rug to get a closer look at the photographs that catalog our relationship from beginning to end. There is one of the two of us at a fancy seafood restaurant, celebrating the anniversary of our first date. Our wedding photo: me wearing a white lacy gown, with my vivid crimson hair pulled up into a French twist, little tendrils falling around the side of my face, and Grant looking devastatingly handsome in a tuxedo. Another photo of our honeymoon in Cancun, looking happy and tan on the beach.

"You must be missing him a lot."

Poppy's voice comes from behind me, and I nearly jump out of my skin. I turn around to find her holding out a steaming mug of tea. I take it so as not to be rude, and now I have to stand here, holding this gross tea, pretending to drink it.

You would think that if Poppy is my closest friend, she would know I don't enjoy drinking tea. There is, in fact, quite a lot she doesn't know about me.

"Drink up while it's hot," she tells me.

Obligingly, I take a sip of the tea. Not surprisingly, it's terrible. Because it's tea.

Poppy sits beside me and idly picks up the paperback book I've got lying on the coffee table. She reads the description and flips through the pages. "*The Boyfriend...* Is this any good?"

"Oh, yes—I love it. But I'm on page two, and I'm

pretty sure I already know what the twist is going to be." I take another tentative sip of tea. "Have you ever heard of the author, Freida McFadden?"

"Nope."

"She writes psychological thrillers. The kind with short chapters and lots of twists that are shocking but also kind of completely out of nowhere."

"Still nope." She hesitates. "Oh, wait. Did she write *Fifty Shades of Grey*?"

"Uh, no."

"*Harry Potter*?"

"No."

"Then no, never heard of her. What else did she write?"

"She wrote this one thriller novella that was supposed to be satirical."

"*Satirical*? What does *that* mean?"

"Like, it makes fun of other thrillers in a way that's supposed to be over the top and funny."

Poppy frowns thoughtfully. "Was it actually funny?"

"Eh. If you like that sort of thing." I shrug. "Oh! She also wrote *The Housemaid*."

"Housemaid? Is she British?" Poppy asks.

"Oh, I'm not sure. Yes, probably."

Poppy tosses the paperback back on the table. I pretend to take another sip of tea while she gets up to study the photos on my mantel. She scrutinizes them one by one, a frown spreading across her lips. "You guys were so happy together. This must be so hard for you."

You have no idea, Poppy, I want to tell her. *It's so hard that I'm seeing Grant while I'm buying shampoo.*

"Yes," I say instead.

"Sometimes I think we all just get a certain amount of happiness," she muses. "And you and Grant had so much of it during your time together. Maybe you simply… used it all up."

Great theory, Poppy. I force a smile. "I was certainly blessed."

"And it might not have seemed like it at the time," she says, "but it ended up being a good thing that you never got pregnant, even though I know you and Grant had been hoping for it."

I close my eyes for a moment, thinking of all those extra bedrooms upstairs. Grant had a twinkle in his eyes when we talked about turning one of them into a nursery, but then every month, I would get my period, and there would be that unspoken disappointment.

I press the palm of my hand against my abdomen.

"I just want you to know," Poppy says, "that you're my best friend, and whatever you need, I am here for you."

But I'm not listening to Poppy. I'm looking over her shoulder, at the window that overlooks the side of our house and the narrow and deserted path that runs between my house and Poppy's. The two houses are divided by a picket fence that surrounds my entire property.

For a split second, I could swear there is a face staring at me through that window.

3

After Poppy goes home, I climb the spiraling staircase, which creaks and groans with each step, until I reach the second floor.

I never go higher than that—I haven't ventured even once up to the attic, which contains a single room that locks from the outside. Grant says the room is used as storage for items that belonged to his late wife, Rebertha, who lived here before me and died in a tragic accident long before we met. I don't even have the key.

As I pad through the hallway, a sound comes from up above. During the time we have lived in this house, I have often heard mysterious noises—thumps and moans and once something that sounded very much like a scream but Grant insisted was the wind. He explained that these are normal "house sounds," and I just don't understand because I've never lived in an old house before.

I stop short as the ceiling trembles with another

thump from up above. The noise sounded very much like footsteps. Is somebody up there? Is that possible?

No, it couldn't be.

I push away thoughts of the mysterious attic room which I was never allowed to enter and continue to the master bedroom. Even though Grant is gone, I still sleep on the right side of the bed. I can't seem to break that habit even now that I have a whole king-sized bed to stretch out on. Every night since his death, I have jolted awake several times, expecting to see him sleeping soundly on the mattress beside me. But his side of the bed is always empty.

The bed still smells like him. The sheets have been changed twice since his death, yet the scent of him lingers. The whole room smells like his sandalwood cologne.

I wish I had something in my life to take my mind off the death of my husband. I gave up my job as a real estate agent soon after Grant and I married. At first, I was reluctant to give it up. But he talked me into it.

"My job is my life," I remember telling him.

"But you don't need a job," he insisted. "I have more than enough money to take care of the two of us for several lifetimes. My job is to make you happy, and if I'm doing it right, you should never have to work."

And when he looked into my eyes, I believed he meant it. He tried so hard to make me happy. He said he loved the way my eyes lit up when he gave me presents, which was something he did with great frequency. He loved to spoil me.

Giving up my job was something I came to regret.

After a while, all the days started to feel the same. I was bored. There was more to life than watching television and shopping and book club meetings. But I tried to be the perfect little wife, hoping to please him.

In the middle of the afternoon, I got the phone call. It was the police, telling me about a terrible car accident on the Long Island Expressway. There was only one victim—my husband—and they needed me to identify his body. I drove down to the morgue as fast as I could, narrowly avoiding an accident myself. In spite of how mangled he was, it took me five seconds to positively identify my husband. I knew that face very well.

"I'm so sorry," the police officer told me as I wiped away the single tear that was rolling down my cheek.

This must have been how Grant felt when Rebertha died in that awful accident at sea.

I try to block out the memory of that fateful day as I open the walk-in closet of the bedroom. The left half is stuffed with Grant's suits for work. I run my fingers along the expensive fabric of one of the dark ones. I never thought there was much difference between a cheap and an expensive suit, but Grant taught me other-wise. He always loved to look his best.

And then there's my side of the closet on the right. Grant insisted I get rid of all the outfits from the before time—before Grant came into my life, when everything I wore was purchased on sale from the discount rack. He bought me all new clothes with labels like Givenchy and Prada and Gucci.

And stuffed at the far end of the row of dresses is the one dress I will never forget. It taunts me, innocently dangling from that hanger. I run my fingers along the smooth fabric, my heart pounding all the way up in my throat.

No. I will not think about that dress anymore. That time in my life is officially over.

I flick off the lights in the closet. Same as downstairs in the hall closet, the lights overhead are LEDs. Grant never understood why I insisted on installing them. If he'd known the reason, he never would have agreed.

I close my eyes, remembering the reflection of Grant's face in the mirror of the sunglasses display. At the moment, it seemed so incredibly real. But now that I'm looking back on it, how could it have been? Grant is *dead*. I identified his body at the morgue. I attended his funeral, where they lowered his coffin into the ground and buried him six feet under. The only way I could have seen him is if he were a ghost, and I would be so mad if that happened, because it would seriously be a super-cheap twist.

I must have imagined it. After all the trauma I have been through, it's not entirely surprising that I would imagine I'm seeing Grant's face, even when he's clearly not really there.

The herbal tea that I forced myself to drink is sloshing around in my bladder. My next stop is the master bathroom, with its heated floors and toilet seat. Heated floors and toilet seats are some of the things I never knew I needed in my life until I had them. If heaven exists, I guarantee every bathroom has heated toilet seats and toasty-warm floors. Although I can't be sure that's where I'm going.

The toilet flushes automatically when I stand up. It's quite a special toilet—I can't emphasize that enough. As I wash my hands in the sink, I catch a glimpse of an object lying in the small wastepaper basket next to the toilet, and my stomach clenches.

One week ago, I pulled that test strip out of its wrapper. I sat on the heated toilet seat and watched the two blue lines appear that would change my life forever.

I'm pregnant.

4

I WAKE UP THE NEXT MORNING TO THE WHIR OF THE vacuum cleaner. I always felt capable of doing my own cleaning, but Grant loved to spoil me, so he insisted on hiring someone to do this job. And I have to admit, it's nice having a person to clean my floors, swap out the sheets on the beds, and wash the dishes.

Since they will want to clean inside the master bedroom, I shower quickly, throw on a sweater and designer jeans, then head downstairs. When I get to the first floor, the smell of eggs and bacon wafts into my nostrils. I reach the dining room just in time to see the plate containing my breakfast being placed on the huge mahogany table large enough to seat twelve.

"Hello, Mrs. Lockwood," a familiar voice says.

I force a smile onto my lips to greet Willie, our houseman. "Hello."

"I have your full breakfast prepared," Willie tells me in an accent that I've never quite been able to identify. "It's nothing too fancy. Just some bacon, sausages, eggs, black pudding, baked beans, tomatoes, mushrooms, toast, fried bread…" He pauses. "And of course, a cup of tea."

"Thank you, Willie," I say. "It smells absolutely delicious."

"I hope you like it, Mrs. Lockwood."

I meet Willie's eyes across the dining table. Willie is in his late twenties, with a shock of jet-black hair, and there's something incredibly alluring about him. I'm not sure exactly what it is. Maybe it's his dark, dark eyes or his broad, muscular shoulders. Maybe it's the fact that he always cleans our house with his shirt off. It's hard to put my finger on it, but Grant never entirely trusted him.

"Is there anything else I can do for you, Mrs. Lockwood?" he asks me. "Anything at all?"

"No, thank you."

"I'll get back to work, then."

Willie grabs a bottle of lemon-scented spray and strides over to the living room to clean our coffee table. I settle down before my plate of food, making sure I have a view of Willie as he bends over to clean the table.

In the weeks before Grant's death, he urged me to fire Willie and find a new houseman. "There's something off about him," Grant used to say.

He would have trusted him even less if he'd known the truth about our houseman's dark past.

5

WHILE I'M AT THE GROCERY STORE THAT AFTERNOON, I discover there are almost as many varieties of prenatal vitamins as there are of shampoo. For example, do I buy the one that has eighteen different vitamins and minerals, including folic acid and DHA? Or do I buy the one that specifically mentions choline? Not that I know what choline is, but if they mention it, it's important, right? Or should I just buy the one that is raspberry lemonade flavored, because I'm always a sucker for raspberry lemonade?

Finally, I grab the vitamins that advertise *advanced brain support*. Because whatever else, I would like my baby's brain to have adequate support.

As I toss the bottle of prenatal vitamins into my shopping cart, I press my palm against my abdomen, which is still flat as a board. It's hard to imagine that there is an actual baby growing inside there. I wouldn't believe it, but pregnancy tests don't lie. It wasn't meant to be this way, but the wild part is now that it happened, I love her more than anything.

I have made mistakes in my life, but I swear, I will make it up to you, baby.

I decided to shop at the grocery store this time, because the drugstore apparently triggers hallucinations of my dead husband. Thankfully, I have been at the supermarket for ten minutes, and there have been zero dead husbands during that time.

Of course, I can't *just* buy prenatal vitamins. That would be like holding up a huge flag for everyone to see that says "I am pregnant." I need to buffer my purchase with other items so as not to call attention to the entire reason I came to the grocery store. I toss several other things into the cart, including a loaf of bread, some cheese, another bottle of shampoo, and—just to *really* throw off the cashier—a package of maxi pads.

I push my shopping cart to the checkout line. Unfortunately, I arrived at the supermarket at the worst possible time, because all the lines have at least four or five people in them. The ten-items-or-less register seems the most promising, so I get in line behind a man who has not followed my buffer rule and is simply clutching a box of ribbed condoms in his right hand with a very singular purpose in mind. He keeps checking his watch.

"Alice! Alice Lockwood! Is that you?"

I curse under my breath at the familiar voice. It's Eliza Bradley, who used to work as Grant's secretary. She's pushing a cart containing nothing but cans of gourmet cat food, and she's wearing a puffy coat that is far too warm for the weather we're having.

"Hello," I mumble, hoping that if I don't look at her, she might get the message that I'm not in the mood for chitchat.

But Eliza is not to be deterred. She pushes her cart so close to mine that they are practically kissing and peers up at me. Her face is wrinkled, and her lips nearly vanish into her mouth. "My dear, I didn't get a chance to talk to you at the funeral. I am so terribly sorry."

Of all the people I could have run into today at the supermarket, she is the last one I wanted to see. "Uh-huh" is all I can manage.

"Grant was such a wonderful man," she continues. "He was a great boss. He was so thoughtful. And charming. And *young*. What a terrible shame."

"Mm-hmm."

"I told Grant that Mercedes of his wasn't safe," she says. "American cars are the safest ones on the market. The only ones that I trust, you know? That's why I've driven a Ford for the last forty years."

"Mm-hmm."

"By the way, Alice," Eliza says. "I hate to be that person, but you *do* realize this is the ten items or less line, don't you?"

"Excuse me?"

"Well…" She points accusingly at the contents of my cart. "You actually have *eleven* items in your cart. I know it's only one over, but ten is the cutoff for a reason. I mean, if we're going to allow eleven, do we say twelve is fine? How about thirteen? Where do we draw the line, Alice?"

"Okay, I get it," I say through my teeth. "I… I'll get rid of one of the items."

"I'd be happy to help you sort through while we're waiting?" Eliza offers.

"No, that's really… That's not…"

But Eliza is already reaching into my cart, rifling through my potential purchases. "I'm sure we can get rid of one of these. Do you really need…" She picks up a box from the cart. "Lice shampoo?"

Oh my God. I did *not* realize that was lice shampoo! Although now that she mentions it, there is a drawing of a dead insect on the bottle. I thought the insect just meant the shampoo was all natural.

"Oops," I say. "You're absolutely right. I don't need lice shampoo. So I'll just put that back…"

But Eliza isn't listening to me. She is looking through the other items in my cart, and now her fingers are resting on the bottle of prenatal vitamins. She lifts her eyes, which are wide with slightly clouded lenses. "Alice, are you…?"

"Oh my gosh!" I clutch my chest in a show of fake surprise. "*Prenatal* vitamins? I thought those were just regular women's multivitamins! What a stupid mistake! They should really label them better!"

"It says prenatal vitamins right on the label in big pink letters," she points out.

I try to laugh. "I just saw *vitamins*."

"And it says for baby brain support."

"I should really read the labels more carefully, shouldn't I?"

"And there's a picture of a pregnant woman on it!"

I yank the bottle of prenatal vitamins out of Eliza's hand, hoping to finally shut her up. "You know what? I'll go put these back. And the lice shampoo. Can you watch my cart please?"

"Yes, I can," Eliza says, "but I can't hold your place in line if your turn comes up."

Of course she can't. "I promise, I'll just be a minute."

I don't know what to do at this point. The prenatal vitamins were the only reason I came to the supermarket in the first place. I don't want to leave without them, but if I get back in line to buy them, Eliza will figure out my secret. And that woman is a huge gossip.

So I do what I have to do. I put back the two items, knowing that I'll have to make a second trip later to purchase the vitamins. It's worth it to keep my private business from being spread all over town. And anyway, I can only purchase ten items.

I hurry back to the cashiers to make sure not to lose my place. But as I am approaching the checkout line, my eyes are drawn to the large windows by the exit. When I was standing in line, all I saw through that window was the parking lot outside the store. But now I see something else.

Or should I say, *somebody* else. There's a familiar-looking man standing by the window, his blue eyes staring into the supermarket. He is wearing an expensive business suit, and his blond hair is immaculately styled. His gaze is unmistakably pointed in my direction. And this time, when our eyes meet, he doesn't look away.

It feels like an icy cold hand has gripped my heart

inside my chest. I look over at Eliza, who is flipping through an overpriced magazine she found at the checkout aisle.

"Eliza," I hiss.

She lifts her eyes from a photograph of the royal family. "What's wrong?"

"Do you see that man over there by the windows?"

Eliza squints in the direction that I'm pointing. "Yes…"

"Doesn't he look just like Grant?"

She blinks at me. "Like Grant? What on earth do you mean, Alice? He doesn't look anything like Grant."

I swivel my head back in the direction of the window, ready to plead my case, but then I stop short. There is a man standing in front of the window with a sack of groceries, but he has gray hair and a potbelly. Eliza is right—he doesn't look anything like Grant. But there was another man standing there a minute ago. I'm sure of it.

"I have to go," I gulp.

"But, Alice!" Eliza exclaims. "You can't just leave your cart with all the items! You have to put them all back in the proper locations!"

But I'm not listening to Eliza. I squeeze through the checkout line sans groceries, and I sprint through the automatic doors so quickly they almost don't open in time for me. I finally burst into the parking lot, gasping for air. I search the lot, scanning every row for the man with the expensive business suit and blond hair.

He is nowhere to be seen. But he was here. I am

more certain of that than I have been of anything in my entire life. There was a man standing by that window who looked exactly like Grant. And he was staring straight at me.

6

"YOU SAW *GRANT* IN THE PARKING LOT OF THE supermarket?"

Yes, I cracked and told Poppy. I couldn't help it. It's bad enough that I can't tell anyone I'm pregnant, but I couldn't keep this secret too. So as soon as I got home, I called her to come over. I had to hear what she thought.

So far, she seems to think I've gone off the deep end.

"It sounds really wild," I say, "but I know my husband's face."

"Yes…" Poppy shifts on the sofa next to me. "I don't doubt that. But there are a lot of men out there who resemble Grant. Maybe from far away, you thought…"

"But he was staring at me," I insist. "I'm sure of it."

Poppy doesn't believe me. And I can't entirely blame her, since I can't come up with one explanation for how I could be seeing my husband at the grocery store when he is, in fact, buried in the ground.

And we definitely buried him. I distinctly remember

standing by his grave, surrounded by friends and relatives, dabbing the tears from my eyes with a lace handkerchief. I remember his coffin being lowered into the ground.

And we buried him in a *normal* cemetery. We didn't bury him in some special *pet* cemetery where he would come back to life after a week or two, carrying a terrible curse. Grant was buried in a regular cemetery where nobody comes back to life. Which means he's dead and in the ground.

I'm one hundred percent sure.

Well, okay, I guess not one hundred percent.

While Poppy is trying to figure a nice way to tell me I've lost my mind, Willie emerges from the kitchen, carrying a mug brimming with herbal tea. He is still shirtless, his taut muscles rippling under his deeply tanned and glistening skin.

"Here is your tea, Miss Lockwood," Willie says.

I accept the mug, but the smell of it turns my stomach. I've been noticing that smells make me more nauseated than they used to. I wonder how long I'll be able to conceal my pregnancy.

"Can I do anything else for you?" he asks me. "Anything… at all?"

There's a glint in his dark eyes that makes me shiver deliciously. Willie is devastatingly handsome, and now that my husband is no longer around, what would be the harm in showing a little interest?

But no. Willie is the last person I would want to get involved with. I know exactly what sort of person he is and what he's capable of, and while it's fine for him to clean my home, it would be a dangerous game to allow anything else to happen.

"I'm fine," I assure him. "Thank you."

Poppy follows Willie's progress with her eyes as he makes his way back into the kitchen. "That houseman of yours," she says. "He's really something."

"That's for sure."

She smiles shyly. "Do you think he might be willing to be *my* houseman too?"

I don't answer her question, partially because I'm fighting back a wave of nausea and partially because despite his appearance, she wouldn't *actually* want Willie to be her houseman. Not if she knew about his prison record.

Poppy pauses, and I notice she's staring down at my throat. I shift uncomfortably.

"That's a lovely necklace, Alice," she tells me.

My fingers fly to the chain around my neck, which has a snowflake pendant hanging off it. "Thank you."

"Have you worn that before? I feel like I saw you wear that snowflake necklace on another occasion."

"Well, yes, I'm sure I've worn it before."

"It's just strange to me." She cocks her head to the side. "The *same* snowflake necklace two different times. On two separate occasions. What does it mean?"

I frown. "Nothing."

"But there must be some sort of meaning or symbolism…"

"No. I'm just wearing the same necklace twice—that's all." I fiddle with my necklace, almost wanting to take it off just so she'll stop asking me about it. Sheesh.

"Are you okay?" Poppy asks.

I shoot her a look. She's seriously asking me that? Not only has my husband died in a fiery car wreck, but now I am seeing him at the grocery store. Does she really need to ask me if I'm okay? I am so clearly not okay.

"I mean," she says quickly, "you look a little green."

I have been keeping my nausea under wraps, but the second she points it out, it becomes overwhelming. I clamp a hand over my mouth and dash off to the kitchen as quickly as I can. I lean over the sink and vomit up everything I ate for lunch.

As I am bent over the sink, waiting to see if more is coming, Poppy's footsteps behind me grow louder. As I straighten up, I find her standing behind me, staring at me with her mouth hanging open.

"Alice?" she says.

I'm pregnant.

I almost blurt out the words. Poppy is my best friend, and I'm desperate to tell her the truth. And I surely would have, except at that moment, the doorbell echoes throughout the house. Wow, literally saved by the bell.

"I'd better get that," I say.

I at least have the wherewithal to gargle a little bit of water to rinse the vomit taste out of my mouth. Poppy hangs back in the kitchen while I tuck the strands of flaming-red hair behind my ears and pad over to the front door. I check the peephole, and for a moment, I am absolutely convinced that Grant will be standing there in one of his Armani suits, his Berluti leather briefcase clutched in his right hand.

But thank God, it's not him. Instead, it's a woman wearing a wool coat over a simple flower-print dress. She looks harmless enough, so I unlock the door.

The woman standing before me is about my height and build—she actually looks a bit like me. Her hair is a shade or two darker, but she has a similar nose and mouth and coloring. Someone could mistake us for sisters, or if not that, at least cousins.

"Hello," I say politely. "Can I help you?"

She stands there, wringing her hands together. I wonder if she's selling something. She doesn't have anything with her that looks like it could be for sale, but perhaps it's in a catalog. Or maybe she's selling magazine subscriptions.

Ooh, or maybe it's Girl Scout cookies. I hope that's what it is. I love Thin Mints.

"Hello," she says. "Are you Alice Lockwood?"

"Yes…" I say.

"And Grant Lockwood is…" She pauses. "Grant Lockwood *was* your husband?"

"Yes." I frown, suddenly wishing I had not opened the door for this strange woman. The chances of her pulling out a box of Thin Mints is decreasing by the second. "What is this all about? Who are you?"

"My name is Marnie." She looks me straight in the eyes. "And I am Grant Lockwood's wife."

7

WHAT?

For a full twenty seconds, all I can do is stare at this woman. *I am Grant Lockwood's wife.* No matter how many times it repeats in my head, it still doesn't make sense.

"That can't be," I say like the woman is a child who needs the concept of marriage to be explained to her. "*I* am Grant Lockwood's wife. And you can only have one wife."

"I… I wasn't his legal wife," Marnie says. "But we lived together as man and wife for many years."

This is the most ridiculous thing I've ever heard. Grant could not possibly have been living an entirely separate secret life with this other woman, who happens to look a lot like me. Who has *time* for something like that?

"Grant told me he didn't believe in marriage," she says in a voice tinged with bitterness. "I had no idea about you, of course. I was about to call the police because Grant hadn't come home the night before, and then… then I saw his obituary in the paper." She chokes on her words, her eyes welling with tears. I almost start to comfort her, but then I stop myself. "The obituary mentioned your name and… well, here I am."

I don't know what to say to that. I don't believe that Grant was living two lives. It's simply not possible.

"Why are you telling me this?" I ask.

Her lips turn down, which ages her face. I had thought she was about my age, but now I would judge her to be several years older—close to forty. "Grant died, and because you are his legal wife, you inherit all his substantial assets. I get nothing."

Okay, now I get it. The chick wants money.

"I'm sorry," I say stiffly. "I don't know what kind of scam this is, but Grant only had *one* wife, and that's me. Whatever went on between the two of you—if anything —it was clearly in the past. It has nothing to do with me or my husband anymore. Legally, you're not entitled to one red cent."

I put my hand on the door, preparing to close it in Marnie's face. But before I can, she spits out the words that make me freeze in my tracks: "Grant and I… We had children together."

8

WHAT? MARNIE HAS *CHILDREN* WITH GRANT? NOT JUST a child, but *children*—plural.

My legs tremble beneath me, and my nausea returns full force. I would be running back to the sink if there were anything left in my stomach.

"You're lying," I manage.

She shakes her head sadly. "He told me he had accounted for his family in his will, but then I discovered that there was no will. Everything went to you. And meanwhile, we are struggling not to lose our home."

I have no words. If this woman really is telling the truth—if Grant really did father children with her and she had no idea about my existence—then they do deserve part of his vast estate. But I'm having trouble comprehending this truth. Grant did work long hours at his business and even traveled a fair amount, but I still don't understand how he could have had a whole other family on the side.

"Here, let me show you something." Marnie digs

into her purse and pulls out her phone. She scrolls through the screen, and when her fingers pause, she passes me the phone. "That's the two of us together."

I stare at the image on the screen of her phone, my eyes widening in disbelief. It's a picture of Marnie and Grant with their cheeks pressed together, smiling wide for the camera—the ultimate selfie. I could believe that the man that I saw at the drugstore or the supermarket wasn't my husband, but there's no debating who is in this photo. It's Grant.

And that bastard always told me he hated selfies.

Marnie swipes the screen again, and an image appears of Grant holding a toddler. He is very much the proud father, and the little towheaded boy in his arms bears a striking resemblance to my husband.

I don't even understand how it's possible. We ate dinner together at least four or five nights of the week. When he told me he was taking a brief stroll around the neighborhood after dinner, was he actually going out to have dinner with an entirely different family?

But just because the photo appears real, that doesn't mean it is. This could all be an elaborate lie. Photoshop does incredible things these days.

"You still don't believe me," she says.

"It's a bit hard to wrap my head around," I admit.

She plucks her phone out of my hands and drops it into her purse. I can't help but notice that while my purse is a Gucci original, hers is made of cloth and looks like it might have been constructed by the toddler in the photograph.

"Would you like to meet the kids?" she asks.

My gut is telling me not to get in a car with this woman. It's possible she's telling the truth, but it's also possible she is entirely unhinged. What if the second we're alone, she takes me hostage?

As if reading my mind, she adds, "We can take separate cars. I'll give you my address."

I don't know what to do. This could be a trap, but at the same time, Marnie doesn't seem dangerous. Her grief appears genuine. "I don't know…"

She scribbles her address on a scrap of paper from her purse and hands it over to me. "Please come, Alice. If you loved Grant, I hope you wouldn't want his offspring to go hungry."

She watches my face, waiting for an answer. When it comes down to it, she is absolutely right. "No," I say, "I wouldn't."

"Thank you," she says. "I know you'll do the right thing."

With those words, she shows herself out.

9

After Marnie is gone, I lean against the door, my entire body shaking. Poppy, who made herself scarce during my conversation with Marnie, joins me in the foyer, her astonished expression mirroring the way I'm feeling. Her mouth is open so wide it looks like her jaw might unhinge.

"You're not actually thinking about going to that lunatic's house, are you?" Poppy asks.

"The photos looked real…"

"So what?" she retorts. "Alice, they can fake anything these days. Videos, voices… You can't trust a couple of photographs."

"Right. That's why I need to go there and see for myself."

"Please don't go, Alice. Just sit down for a minute and think this over. I'll make you another cup of tea."

"I don't need to think it over."

"I have a really bad feeling about this." She shivers, even though the temperature in this room is a perfect seventy-four degrees. We have the ability to make every room in this house a specific different temperature, using only an app on my phone. "I'm scared that woman could be dangerous. And you keep telling me you're being followed…"

"But not by a woman."

"It's still very creepy."

She's right. If somebody is following me, their reasons for doing so must be unsavory. Whoever has been following me around wants to hurt me.

But at the same time, now that Marnie has dropped this bombshell on me, I can't think of anything else. I need to know if Grant really was leading a secret life with another family.

"I'm sorry, Poppy," I say to her. "I have to go to her house. I have to know if what she was telling me is true."

10

The address Marnie gave me is only a twenty-minute drive away. Even though it's geographically close, as I drive through the streets of her neighborhood, I immediately recognize that I have entered a different social class. This is not the kind of neighborhood that I live in, where houses have heated toilets and skylights and newly renovated kitchens and temperature control using phone apps. This is a neighborhood where you don't want to venture out after dark.

I locate Marnie's house using my GPS, and when I pull up in front of the two-story cottage, I can't help but think how much shabbier her house is than mine. If she is the mother of Grant's children, why does she have a house that looks like it's crumbling at the foundations, while I have a house that contains something called a smart refrigerator?

I step out of my Lexus, which is a great deal nicer than the old, dented Kia parked in the driveway. As I start up the walkway to the front door, once again, I get the feeling somebody is watching me. This time, it's so strong that it stops me in my tracks.

I turn around. The street is quiet right now. There's a man down the block who is mowing his lawn, but other than that, nobody is there. Certainly, nobody is watching me.

And then I see a slight rustling in the bushes on the periphery of the lawn. I watch them, certain that my husband will emerge from the shrubbery at any moment, possibly in zombie form. But I stand there for at least sixty seconds, and there is no further movement. Nobody is coming out of the bushes to talk to me or eat my brains. Nobody is there at all.

Maybe it was the wind.

I turn around and continue my journey to the front door. I press my finger against the doorbell, but I don't hear any sound. It must be broken. So instead, I bang my fist against the door.

I hear bursts of crying in several different pitches. There is a large amount of shuffling behind the door, and several seconds later, Marnie pulls it open, still wearing that same floral-print dress but this time with a milk stain on the front. A baby of about one year old is balanced on one of her hips.

When Marnie sees me, her face breaks into a tired smile. "Alice!" she cries. "You came."

"Yes…."

I don't know what to make of this. Is this child on Marnie's hip really Grant's offspring? Admittedly, he does resemble my husband, but it's hard to find features of a thirty-seven-year-old man on the face of an infant. I still don't know what to believe.

"I know this must be weird for you," she acknowledges. "It's weird for me too. I had no idea there was another woman in Grant's life. But we both know that Grant would not have wanted his family to starve."

It takes all I have to keep myself from blurting out, "But I thought I was his only family."

Grant was an only child, and his parents died long before we met. It was one of the reasons he so badly wanted us to have a child of our own. He had no family, and he desperately wanted to start one with me. I had no idea that he already had a head start with somebody else.

"Please," Marnie says. "Won't you come in?"

I obediently follow her into the living room. I expected to see another child playing in there, but that's not what I see. There are, in fact, so many children in this room that I'm having trouble counting them all. There is a teenage girl on the sofa who has a sour expression on her face as she scrolls on her phone. There's one child who appears to be writing *Ayah* on the wall. There's a child of about four years old who is wearing only a pair of underwear and eating a bowl of chocolate ice cream from his lap while he sits on an armchair.

"That's Michaela on the sofa—always on her phone." Marnie gives me a conspiratorial look as if I'm intimately familiar with the relationship between the teenage progeny of my husband and their phones. "Then that's Deacon eating the ice cream. Ember is the one making snow angels on the carpet. Royce is the one spinning around in a circle. Ayah is the one who is— Ayah, stop writing on the wall! And then over on the dining table are Shyleigh and Skyla. And then this one on my hip is little Arlo." She beams at the baby. "Say hi to the nice lady, Arlo."

Arlo sucks on his thumb.

I'm at a loss for words. I accepted that there was a tiny possibility my husband could have had a child or two with this woman. But there are enough children in this room to become a pop band of siblings that tours around the country in a psychedelic school bus. How could these children all be the spawn of my late husband?

Yet they undeniably look like him. They all have his blond hair and his eyes and his facial structure. Not only that, but the walls are littered with framed photographs of Marnie and Grant with their children. If this is a hoax, it is an extremely elaborate one.

Deacon eats the last spoonful of his chocolate ice cream and runs over to his mother. He tugs on her dress and looks up at her with his chocolate-smeared face. "Mommy, is Daddy coming home soon?"

Marnie glances over at me and then gives her son a crooked smile. "He's been very busy traveling, honey. It might be a while before he comes home again."

"Mommy," he says again, "will we get to eat dinner tonight? My tummy was so empty at bedtime last night."

How could he be so hungry when he was literally just eating ice cream? But the kid does look almost skeletal. In fact, the entire family appears a bit malnourished, including Marnie.

"I hope so, Deacon," Marnie replies. "It's up to Auntie Alice over here."

"Mommy," he continues.

Oh God, what now?

"Do you think we'll be able to watch television tonight, or will the power get shut off again?"

"Don't worry," she says. "Even if the lights go out, we can have another sleepover with flashlights. Wasn't that fun?"

This kid is going to make me burst into tears. If Marnie's goal was to pull my heartstrings, she has successfully achieved it. I can't leave this house without helping these poor children.

"Fine," I finally say. "I'll make sure you get a piece of Grant's inheritance."

Her eyes light up. "Really?"

"We would need to do a DNA test, though. You know that, right?"

"Of course, of course…"

"If it comes back as a match," I say, "I will arrange to give you half of the insurance and inheritance money."

Her face fills with fury, pink circles appearing on her cheeks. "Half?" she bursts out. "Do you *see* how many children are in this room? It costs me a week's salary just to pay for one night of dinner! And you…" She wrinkles her nose. "It's just *you*. All you have to worry about is yourself."

"Actually…" I lay one hand on my abdomen protectively. "I'm pregnant."

It's the first time I have uttered those words out loud. Marnie might not be my friend, like Poppy is, but we are connected. After all, when I have a child, that child will be a half-sibling to her children. Marnie and I are family now.

"So what?" Marnie shoots back. "So am I!"

Seriously? How many children was my husband planning to have with this woman before I found out about it?

But I can't blame Marnie. She was in the dark, just like me. I can't let her family starve just because my husband was a shit.

"Let me see what I can do," I tell her.

11

WHILE I'M DRIVING HOME, I NOTICE THE DARK-GREEN sedan. I'm not the sort of person who would ordinarily notice a car trailing me. For all I know, every time I have left the house for the last decade, there has been someone following me. But lately, I am on high alert. Plus, the car has a pair of dice hanging from the rearview mirror, which makes it recognizable even from a few car lengths back.

For the first fifteen minutes of the drive, I try to convince myself it's all a coincidence. Yes, a green car with dice hanging from the rearview mirror is riding my bumper at every turn. But that doesn't mean they're following me. Maybe they're just coincidentally going to the exact same place that I'm going.

Then I get creative. I'm only about five minutes away from my house, but instead of swinging left at the light to get home, I turn right. I check my rearview mirror, blessedly dice free, to see if the green car is still there or if they have turned in a different direction. But there it is—the green car, still behind me.

I signal to turn left, but instead take another right. Again, I check the mirror after the turn. Those white dice with the black spots are swinging behind me.

I take another right. And another.

I have now done a complete circle, yet the car with the dice in the window is still behind me. This can't be a coincidence anymore. There is no way another car just decided to take a turn around an entire block. Whoever is in the green sedan is definitely following me.

I reach over to press the button to lock all the doors on my Lexus as I skid to a stop at another crimson light. I raise my eyes to look in my rearview mirror, adjusting it slightly so that I can see directly through the windshield of the car behind me.

The dice sway slightly. The driver of the car is wearing a large pair of black sunglasses that obscure half his face, although I can plainly see that he is a man with dark-blond hair and chiseled features. Just like my husband.

And then he takes off his sunglasses. Our eyes meet in my rearview mirror. His are clear and blue and achingly familiar. They are Grant's eyes. I have never been so sure of anything in my life.

A loud honk blasts me out of my thoughts. The light has turned green, and somebody behind me is angry that I have waited a single millisecond before taking my foot off the brake. I move through the green light, my head spinning. I make it another half a block, and then I pull over on the side of the road. I check the rearview mirror, expecting to see the green sedan pulling over behind me.

But it is not there. I shift my entire body around, trying to get a good look out the back window. The car is gone. It was behind me for almost twenty minutes, and the second I confirmed that it was following me and was almost positive the man behind the wheel was my husband, the car took off.

I don't understand what's going on. But one way or another, I am getting to the bottom of this.

12

I WAS PLANNING TO DRIVE HOME, BUT INSTEAD, I TAKE A detour. I drive to an entirely different location—a place I last visited two weeks earlier, and until five minutes ago, I had no intention of ever returning to.

It takes me another twenty minutes behind the wheel. It's hard to drive when my thoughts are racing through my skull. I turn on the radio to try to calm myself, but the loud pop music just makes me more agitated. I attempt to find an easy-listening station, but I eventually give up and turn it off entirely.

After what feels like far longer than twenty minutes, I reach my destination. I step out of my Lexus and stand there, gazing at the steel bars in front of me, not wanting to go inside but knowing it's the only way I'll find peace.

I hate cemeteries.

I hug my jacket close to my chest, square my shoulders, and then enter the gates to the cemetery where I buried my husband two weeks earlier. Despite the chill I get when I think about what is lying beneath the ground, it is quite a pretty cemetery. The undertaker showed me photographs when we were planning the funeral, and I knew Grant would approve of the rows of pristine white graves surrounded by plush green grass. The periphery of the cemetery is dotted with bright-red roses, and an immaculate walking path allows visitors to easily traverse the cemetery without trampling the grass.

When the undertaker sold me the plot, he asked if I would like to buy two adjacent plots so that someday I might rest in peace beside my husband.

"No," I told him. "No need for that."

The echo of my heels clacking against the ground sounds like thunderbolts in the quiet cemetery. There are a handful of other living people here, visiting the graves of their relatives, but most of the visitors are quiet. I suppose a cemetery isn't a place for boisterous conversation.

The undertaker sold me plot number eighty-six. That has little meaning when I'm looking out at the rows and rows of nearly identical gravestones. But I remember where they laid my husband to rest. It's hard to forget.

I take the walking path to the middle of the cemetery. A slight breeze is tickling my neck, and once again, I get the distinct feeling somebody is watching me. But of course, that's why I'm here.

I diverge from the paved path and start walking through the grass. I traverse the green blades, my heels digging into the dirt with each step. It takes me another few minutes to find it, but it's not hard since I purchased a more elaborate headstone than most of the other ones here. We did, after all, have money to spare. Of course, I had no idea, when I bought this headstone, that I would soon be providing for the future of Grant's eight—and a half—illegitimate children.

And now I have arrived at the polished black granite headstone. The words etched into the stone read *In loving memory of Grant Lockwood.*

Below the words are the year of his birth and the year of his death and underneath, in script letters, *Loving husband of Alice.*

Nice touch, right?

I stare at the gravestone for much too long as a cool breeze lifts my hair from the back of my neck and the loose strands dance in the wind. This is the same headstone that was here when we buried Grant two weeks ago. Nothing has changed since then.

I drop my gaze to my feet. The grass is intact, right where it was replaced after Grant's coffin was lowered into the ground. I stare at the grass, half expecting a hand to suddenly rip through the soil and wrap its fingers around my ankle.

But no zombie hands are coming out of the ground. Grant is staying put in his coffin. Unless…

It was a closed coffin. We made that decision because of how badly Grant's body was mangled in the accident. But my point is, I never actually saw my husband lying in his coffin. What if it was empty?

But how could that be? Such a thing would surely be noticed. If a body just up and walked out of the morgue, they wouldn't just shrug it off. I certainly hope not, at least.

I fix my gaze on the ground one more time. I am seized with the sudden urge to grab the shovel I keep in my trunk in case of snow and start digging. If I could get to that coffin, I could verify that Grant's body is inside. And if I could do that, I would know that it is not, in fact, my husband who is following me.

But I'm being paranoid now. It's obviously not Grant who is following me. Grant is *dead*. He is absolutely dead. I saw his dead body, and even though I'm not a doctor, it was pretty clear from looking at him that he was very, very dead. And it's a good thing he is.

Because I'm the one who killed him.

And if he were still alive, he would be *pissed*.

13

I know. We seemed like the perfect couple, didn't we?

And we *were* the perfect couple. For a long time, we had that fairy-tale romance little girls dream about. The kind of romance where I sometimes pinched myself because I was sure that it had to be a dream.

Grant claimed that when he first saw me, he knew that he wanted me to be his wife. The truth is, I felt the same way about him. It was as close to love at first sight as I had ever imagined. He was so incredibly handsome, with those gold highlights in his hair, the perfectly chiseled features, the blue, blue eyes like the waters of Aruba —it was hard not to fall madly in love with him. And that was before I discovered he was also successful and wealthy and funny to boot. He was perfect.

On our first date, he took me to a French restaurant. I had never been to such a fancy place in my entire life, but he was not patronizing when he ordered for the two of us. He held my hands across the candlelit table and told me that I looked so beautiful. It was a magical evening, and truth be told, I fell completely in love with him that night, even though I was trying not to.

As we walked out of the restaurant, I noticed him looking at me out of the corner of his eye with a strange expression on his face. "What?" I asked.

"I think," he said, "that I'm not sure I can make it home without kissing you."

I couldn't help but smile at his statement. "Oh?"

"Yes. The fact that I failed to kiss you will quickly consume all my thoughts. I won't even be able to focus on the road when I'm driving home. I'll surely get into a terrible accident."

Nobody had ever expressed to me that they were so consumed by thoughts of me that they could think of nothing else. "Well, I wouldn't want you to get *hurt*."

"You are so kind, Alice," he said as he pressed his lips against mine.

It was like a tiny atomic bomb had been planted inside every single molecule of my body, and during that kiss, they exploded simultaneously. I had been kissed before but never like *that*. He had feared that he might get in an accident if he failed to kiss me, but after that kiss, I didn't think I'd be able to think of anything else ever again for the rest of my life.

But even after that kiss, I tried my best not to fall in love with Grant Lockwood. I kept telling myself that this was what men like Grant did. They wined and dined you, but after they took you to bed, they quickly lost interest. As I fell deeper and deeper into the hole, I reminded myself of this fact.

Grant was a fling. Nothing more.

About eight months after that first dinner in the French restaurant, when we found ourselves dining in that very same restaurant. I ordered the same chocolate soufflé that I had been dreaming about since that first evening together, and while we were waiting for it to rise sufficiently in the oven, Grant dropped his napkin on the floor.

"Let me just pick that up," he told me.

I was surprised. Grant wasn't usually clumsy. While he didn't have much time for sports with his busy schedule, he had a natural athletic grace. Stumbling or dropping things wasn't par for the course for my boyfriend. But a second later, he was on the floor—except it wasn't to pick up his napkin. Grant was down on one knee.

"Alice." He gazed into my eyes as the woman sitting at the table next to ours gawked at us with palpable jealousy. "These last eight months with you have been the best of my life. I would be honored if you would make me the happiest man alive. Will you marry me, Alice?"

I had a huge lump in my throat that made it difficult to talk. But all I needed to get out was one syllable. "Yes!"

The wedding took place six months later. Neither of us had much family, so we decided not to make it a big affair. Then we moved into his big, sprawling house with the five bedrooms, planning to fill them with children.

I had never been so happy in my entire life. No, Grant wasn't absolutely perfect—he worked long hours,

and I didn't get to see him as much as I would have liked
—but he was very much the man of my dreams. Every
night, I fell asleep wondering what I had done to get so
lucky.

I had no idea my husband was a monster.

14

I STILL REMEMBER THE DAY EVERYTHING CHANGED.

It was nearly a year after we were married. We were sitting together on the love seat in our living room, as we often did. I was reading a book, and Grant had his laptop resting on his knees.

I believed he was working, but all of a sudden, he poked me in the arm and said, "Alice, what color is this dress?"

I put down my book and looked over his shoulder at the photograph of a short dress with stripes and ruffled sleeves. "It's white and gold."

Grant tossed back his head and laughed. "No, it's actually blue and black."

"It looks white and gold to me."

"How could you think such a thing?" He snorted. "Are you blind, Alice? It's very clearly blue and black."

I shrugged. "I don't know what to tell you. I think it looks white and gold."

The smile quickly faded from his lips, which set into

a straight line. "What is wrong with you? How could you look at this dress and see white and gold?"

"I just… do."

"Well, you need to get your eyes examined, then. Or maybe your brain." There was no trace of humor on his face anymore. We had been together two years, and he'd never spoken that way to me before. "This is unacceptable. I can't believe I'm married to a woman who is too stupid to tell the difference between white and gold versus blue and black."

"Sorry?"

"Sorry!" he burst out. He flung his laptop onto our overpriced coffee table, and the screen shattered. "That's not an acceptable answer! The dress in that picture is clearly blue and black. I want to hear you say it."

I opened my mouth, but no words came out.

"The dress is blue and black," he spit at me. "I. Want. To. Hear. You. Say. It."

I could only shake my head. "I'll say it if you want. But to me, it does look white and gold."

Grant stared at me, seething with anger. Without another word, he got up off the sofa and stormed out of our home, slamming the door behind him as he left. I could hear his Mercedes zooming away, into the distance.

He didn't return for two days.

I was worried sick. I called the police, but when I told them that he had left of his own accord, they informed me that they would have to wait seventy-two hours to investigate. They were kind to me, though.

They said that it's normal for newlyweds to have little lovers' quarrels. They told me he would probably come home with his tail tucked between his legs and an apology.

And that was exactly what happened. Grant returned home two days later, carrying a huge bouquet of flowers and a gift-wrapped box with my name on it. He encircled me in his arms, and although it took a few moments for me to thaw, I eventually relaxed into his hug. Every couple argued—I supposed in our case, it was just a matter of the honeymoon finally being over.

"The flowers are beautiful," I told him.

"Not as beautiful as you."

I felt a deep sense of relief. Yes, I was still mad at Grant for disappearing for two days, but it was inevitable that Grant and I would have our first fight. It was good to finally get it over with so we could move on with our lives.

Grant thrust the gift box into my hands. "And this is for you as well, my love."

Inside was an ornate white box with a gold ribbon on top. It was so beautiful I almost didn't want to open it. I brought the gift to the sofa and set it down on the coffee table in front of me. I undid the ribbon and carefully lifted the top off the box. My heart skipped a beat when I saw what was inside.

Grant was watching me, a strange expression on his face. "What color is the dress, Alice?"

I peered down at the silk dress folded inside the white box. "It's blue and black," I said numbly.

"Right," he said in a slow voice, like he thought I was stupid. "And what color are the box and ribbon?"

"White and gold."

"Very good. Now do you see the difference?"

I still wonder what would have happened if I had simply agreed with him. But instead, I said, "But the dress in the photo looked different."

"No, it didn't!" Grant was shouting now, loud enough, it seemed, for the whole neighborhood to hear. "The dress in the photo is that exact same dress! You were wrong, Alice. Wrong!"

He grabbed his phone from inside his pants pocket. He unlocked the screen and then shoved the phone into my face. That striped dress was on the screen.

"What color is the dress?" he demanded to know.

"White and gold," I whispered.

"*What color is the dress?*"

I burst into hot tears, which streamed down my cheeks.

My husband's face turned vivid scarlet. He looked as angry as I had ever seen him—as I had ever seen *anyone*. "Put on the dress," he growled.

"I…" I wiped tears from my eyes with the back of my hand. "I'll wear it some other time, okay?"

"If you don't put on that dress," he hissed at me, "I'll have you locked away."

"Locked away?" I stared at him in astonishment. "For what?"

"For hallucinating!" He waved his phone with the picture of the gold-and-white dress. "I could do it if I wanted. The director of the psychiatric ward is my father's brother's nephew's cousin's former college room- mate. He'll do whatever I want him to do—trust me."

I rose from the sofa, my hands clenched into fists. "You can't do that to me. You *can't*."

"I can if you don't do what I tell you!" Now his face was the deep purple of a ripe eggplant. "Put on the dress *right now*!"

I had never been so frightened in my entire life. I ran upstairs to the bedroom and locked the door behind me. He pounded on it, shouting at the top of his lungs. He tried to push the dress through the gap between the door and the floor, but it didn't fit. At one point, I was certain he would break down the door, but he didn't. Eventually, he calmed down.

But it was never the same after that. Grant became relentless. One morning, I opened my closet, and all my outfits had been replaced with blue-and-black dresses. When I would get out of the shower, a blue-and-black dress would be waiting on the bed for me to put on for the day. For my birthday, he gave me a cake with blue icing and the words "Happy Birthday, Alice" spelled out in black letters.

To the entire world, we seemed like the perfect couple. They had no idea what was going on behind closed doors. The rest of the world got bored of debating the color of that dress and moved on to other things, like that BBC guy whose kids burst in during his interview. But for us, the white-and-gold dress had taken over our lives.

Then Grant announced that he wanted to have a baby. When he presented me with a onesie with blue-

and-black stripes, I decided right then and there that I could never bring a child into our marriage. So I took precautions to keep from getting pregnant.

It couldn't go on like this forever, though. Grant was a ticking time bomb. One day, my neighbors would find me strangled in the bathroom with a blue-and-black silk scarf. Before that happened, I had to do something about it.

But Grant would never let me leave. That was one thing I was sure of. I was one of his possessions, and he would never give me up. No, there was only one way to escape my marriage, and that was if one of us was dead.

15

I HAD NEVER KILLED ANYONE BEFORE.

Not to say that I hadn't ever thought about it. We all think of killing someone. That old lady at the checkout line who is paying in pennies from her change purse. The really tall guy who sits in front of you in the movie theater. Basically, every screaming infant on a plane.

But it's only a fantasy. You never do it.

I didn't have a choice with Grant, though. He was a true monster in every sense of the word, and the only way I could escape was to end his life. Really, I would be doing the world a kindness.

Because I had never killed anyone before, I decided to hedge my bets. I mixed hemlock into the orange juice that he drank every morning. I ground up some deadly nightshade to add to the milk he poured on his cereal. I put a banana peel on the top step of our steep staircase. But in the end, it was the cut brake line that did him in.

Still, I was surprised by how easy it was. When the police officer told me to come down to the morgue, I couldn't wrap my head around the fact that my evil husband was actually dead. Even when I stared down at his still body, lying on the slab, his white face rigid, I half expected him to come back to life, clutching a blue-and-black dress in his cold, dead hand.

But Grant didn't come back to life. He was dead. And everyone believed that his car accident was just that —a tragic accident.

The first thing I did after he was gone was throw out all those blue-and-black dresses. I donated most of them to charity, but I saved one. One single dress to remind me of why I'd done what I did.

When I made arrangements for his funeral, I was barely able to believe my husband was gone. I was finally free of that monster. After years of torment, he would never be able to bother me again. I chose a coffin that was white-with-gold trim.

And then, of course, I discovered those two blue lines on the pregnancy test. I had successfully killed my husband, but he had managed to leave a piece of himself behind. I was only relieved that our child would be spared having that man as her father.

Grant is dead. He must be.

But if he is, who is the man who has been following me?

16

Poppy is waiting for me by my front door when I get home from the cemetery, ready to hear the entire sordid tale. Fortunately, she doesn't have a casserole with her.

"What did that woman tell you?" she asks as I unlock my front door.

"I think she's telling the truth. The children… They looked a lot like Grant. And there were photos of the family everywhere."

I don't mention how many kids there were. I still can't quite get over it. The blue-and-black dresses were bad enough, but the eight children I didn't know about are the icing on the cake.

"What a horrible experience," Poppy murmurs. "Can I get you something? How about some tea?"

I just shake my head.

"So, what are you going to do?"

"I… I think I should give her some of the inheritance." I place a hand on my abdomen, knowing that I must save some of the money for the child growing inside me as well. "I'll ask for DNA tests, of course. But if they really are Grant's children, they deserve part of the money."

"I just can't believe it." She shakes her head. "Grant seemed like such a wonderful man. He was so kind and honest and handsome. How could he have been leading a double life?"

You have no idea, Poppy.

"Actually," I find myself saying, "he wasn't as kind and honest as you thought."

She laughs like I made a joke. "What are you talking about? You and Grant were the perfect couple."

"No." I drop my eyes. "We weren't. Our perfect marriage… It was all a lie."

She notices the expression on my face, and the smile slides off her lips. "What do you mean, Alice?"

It's like turning on a faucet, and I can't get it to stop. Before I know it, I have told her everything. About the blue-and-black dress. About… well, that's pretty much all of it. But my God, he was such a jerk about that dress.

Poppy listens to the entire story, her face growing paler. Tears spring to her eyes as I describe the state of my closet.

"You poor thing." She reaches out to clasp my hand. Hers is warm and comforting. "Alice, I had no idea. I wish you had told me. I would have…"

"I couldn't take a chance." I wipe a tear from my own eyes. "What if you thought the dress was blue and black too?"

"Never!" Poppy cries. "That dress was white and gold! Anyone who thought otherwise definitely had defective rods or cones or whatever."

Hearing those words is enough to make me burst into tears. Poppy wraps her arms around me, and we remain in an embrace for several minutes, both of us sobbing our eyes out. I wish I had trusted her enough to come to her sooner. Maybe if I had, I wouldn't have had to kill Grant.

"You know what we really need?" Poppy finally pulls away from me, rubbing her pink nose. "A stiff drink! Let me make us a couple of vodka and tonics."

"You can't," I say miserably. "Because… I'm pregnant."

Poppy gasps. "Alice, I had no idea. You don't look it at all, honestly! How far along are you? Seven months? Eight months?"

I glare at her. "*Six weeks.*"

"Oh." She looks down at my midsection and blinks in surprise. "That's it? Well… okay. If you say so."

"I took precautions to keep it from happening." I let out a wretched sob. "I put LED lights in every closet, but I still got pregnant. I don't understand it."

She cocks her head to the side. "LED lights?"

I nod. "I read online that if you have LEDs placed, they are over ninety-eight percent effective in preventing pregnancy."

Poppy stares at me for several beats, a confused look on her face. "Do you mean… IUDs?"

"What's an IUD?"

"An intrauterine device. A doctor inserts it into your uterus, and it is used to prevent pregnancy."

Wow, that makes *so* much more sense than the lights. Stupid Google search.

"What am I going to do, Poppy?" I wail. "My husband was a monster. Now he's dead, and I've got his child growing inside me. And not only that…" I glance nervously at the window, where I half expect to see Grant's face peering out at me. "I'm seeing him everywhere I go."

"Alice." She squeezes my hand in hers. "You're *not* seeing Grant. Grant is dead, sweetie. This is simply all the stress catching up with you."

I nod, reluctantly accepting that this might be true. I want so badly for it to be true. I need this nightmare to be over.

After Poppy leaves, I try to relax. I decide to go upstairs to take a shower, hoping the scalding-hot water will ease some of my tension. When I get in, I turn the heat up as high as it will go. I still feel tense, so I turn it in the other direction, as cold as it will go.

Just as I'm emerging from the bathroom with a towel wrapped around my chest, the doorbell rings downstairs. God, I hope it's not Poppy with another casserole. I peek out the bedroom window at the driveway, and my heart does a somersault when I see what is waiting downstairs.

It's a police car.

17

I DON'T EVEN HAVE TIME TO DRY MY HAIR. I PULL IT
back into a messy ponytail, then I throw on a pair of
blue jeans and a cardigan. I sprint down the steps as
quickly as possible just as the doorbell rings for a third
time.

When I throw open the door, there's a familiar man
in a shirt and tie paired with a trench coat. I recognize
him as Detective Mancini, who briefly spoke with me
after my husband's tragic accident. He's an older man,
with salt-and-pepper hair that's mostly salt and deep
lines etched into his craggy face.

"Hello there, Mrs. Lockwood." He tips an imaginary
hat in my direction. "I'm so sorry to bother you again.
It's Detective Mancini."

"Yes, I remember you." I force a smile to disguise
the fact that my stomach is doing somersaults. "Is… is
anything wrong?"

Detective Mancini hesitates. When I heard he was
investigating my husband's accident, I asked around and

found that he was a detective who didn't always play by the rules but got the job done. But the last I heard, they had officially ruled Grant's accident just that—an accident.

"Could I come in?" he asks.

I would rather not invite a detective into my home, but if I don't, he might think I have something to hide. So I obligingly step aside. "Of course."

He follows me into the living room, and I offer him a seat on the sofa. He doesn't take his trench coat off when he sits down.

"Could I get you anything?" I ask. "Some tea perhaps? Casserole?"

He shakes his head. "No, thanks."

I settle down in the love seat across from him, my entire body buzzing. "Can I ask what this is about?"

"Well," he says, "we got an anonymous tip. Someone called in and told us they thought the brakes in your husband's Mercedes had been cut. That it wasn't actually an accident."

Someone called and left an anonymous tip? Who would have done such a thing?

And then I think of the man following me around town—the one who looks suspiciously like my dead husband.

"Oh my God!" I cry. "That… that's horrible! I can't believe it could be true…"

"We don't know for sure," Mancini says. "Unfortunately, even though it's against protocol, we didn't check the car after the accident. And now your husband's car has been compounded into one of those cubes at the junkyard. So we can't possibly know if it's really true."

My shoulders relax by a few millimeters. The car has been destroyed. All the evidence is gone.

"But I have to ask you," he says, "did your husband have any enemies? Anyone who might have wanted to hurt him?"

Detective Mancini's left hand has a very light tan line where a wedding ring used to be. I wonder what happened in his own marriage. I wonder if he could possibly understand.

Well, I'll never know. Because I will never tell him the truth.

"He didn't have any enemies," I say, "but there's a man who cleans for us that Grant never entirely trusted."

"You mean Willie, your houseman?"

"That's right." I'm not surprised that the police have already looked into our houseman, which means they have no doubt discovered his dark past. "We hired Willie as a recommendation from another family, so I didn't do a background check. I should have. I never would have hired Willie if I'd known… that he had a prison record."

That's a lie. When we hired Willie, I told Grant that I had done a background check, and that was the truth. I'd discovered his prison record, and that was the very reason I hired him—so that if there was any suspicion about Grant's death, it would fall on our ex-con houseman.

"But I never thought he would hurt Grant." I allow tears to spring to my eyes, laying it on thick. "And besides, despite the terrible thing he did, he put in his time."

"He did do a terrible thing," the detective says.

"I've never met anyone who had over thirty overdue library books before." I grab a tissue from the box on the table and dab at my eyes. "I mean, two or three, yes, I can see how that could happen. Over ten would be bad enough. But over *thirty*?"

"I know." He sighs. "It's the sort of thing you only see once in a lifetime as a cop, and you hope to never see it again."

I sniffle. "How does such a thing happen? I had no idea he was such a... a *monster*. He's clearly capable of anything." Which was exactly why I chose him.

"Yes, I was suspicious too," Mancini says. "That's why I checked him out. And it turns out Willie has an airtight alibi for the day your husband was killed."

My heart does a jumping jack inside my chest. "He... he does?"

He nods. "Yes. He was playing in a Quidditch tournament all day up in Vermont. It was filmed. There's no way he could have been responsible for Grant's accident."

"What?"

"It's true."

"Wait. So Quidditch is an actual *sport*?" I ask incredulously. "And they *film* it?"

"That's right, Mrs. Lockwood," he says solemnly.

"Do they use broomsticks?"

"They do."

I had no idea about any of this. I thought Willie

would take the fall for Grant's murder, and I would be off the hook. His airtight alibi of competing in a Quidditch match is bad news. But on the plus side, I no longer suffer from any attraction to him.

"Anyway…" Detective Mancini rises to his feet. "I won't take up any more of your time, then, Mrs. Lockwood. If we have any more information, I will let you know."

And then, just like that, he's done questioning me. I was certain this would end with me being led from the house in handcuffs, but he doesn't even seem all that suspicious. Thank God they never bothered to check the brakes in the car after the accident for some reason.

I follow the detective to the front door. I am almost weak with relief that he doesn't seem to be suspicious of me and is simply leaving without further discussion. This is finally over, and I'll never have to worry about it again. He places his hand on the doorknob, and just as he's about to turn it, he hesitates.

"Just one more question, Mrs. Lockwood," he says.

"Okay…"

He digs into the pocket of his trench coat and pulls out a Polaroid photo, which he holds out to me. It appears to be a picture of the inside of Grant's wrecked Mercedes, apparently taken before it was compressed into a cube.

"Tell me." he says. "What color is this dress?"

My stomach sinks. I stare at the photo, noticing now that there is a torn dress lying across the back seat of the car. "What?" I manage.

Mancini smiles sheepishly. "I found this photo in

your husband's file, taken from the scene of the accident. And me and the guys at the department can't stop arguing over it. I assume the dress was yours. What color is it? Is it blue and black, or is it gold and white?"

My mouth is too dry to even speak. I part my lips, but no words come out.

"We were just curious," he says.

"It was…" I lick my lips to moisten them. "White and gold, actually."

"Yeah?" He raises his thick black eyebrows. "I thought for sure it was blue and black."

"I… I don't know what to tell you…"

Mancini plucks the photo out of my fingers and tucks it back in his trench coat pocket. "Well, either way, we're going to continue investigating. Your husband's car might be a cube, but I won't rest until I get to the bottom of this. Mark my words."

I watch Detective Mancini get back in his police car and drive away. But even after the car is gone, I still can't relax.

18

After the detective leaves, my head won't stop spinning.

Who called the police to tip them off? Does Mancini suspect I'm the one responsible for Grant's accident? I could see in his eyes that he will stop at nothing until he gets to the truth.

My head is throbbing. I go to the bathroom, in search of something to help dull the pain. I usually take a couple of Tylenol when I have a headache, but Grant has a stronger prescription medication that he used to take when he was having a bad headache. The pill bottle is on the second shelf of the medicine cabinet, and out of desperation, I pluck it off the shelf and unscrew the child safety cap. Then I dump the contents into my left hand.

But there aren't any white pills in the bottle. Instead, the bottle contains something most unexpected. It's a key.

I stare at the small key lying in the palm of my left

hand. I've never seen this key before. It doesn't look like the one to the front door. Or to the mailbox. It's definitely not a car key.

Could it be the key to that room in the attic—the one that only locks from the outside?

Ever since I moved in here, I have wondered what is in that room. Grant insisted that it was just storage, nothing I would be interested in. At one point, he even told me he lost the key. When I suggested getting a locksmith, he snapped at me that there was no point and that I should stay out of the mysterious room in the attic.

But now Grant is dead. At least, I think he is. Either way, he isn't here to stop me.

Gripping the key in my hand, I slowly make my way up the winding staircase to the second floor. I hold onto the banister, knowing that if I have a misstep and fall, it could be hours before anyone finds me. But these steps are nowhere near as steep as the splintery wooden ones leading up to the attic.

When I get to the second floor, another thump comes from above. I've heard it since I have lived here, but Grant always insisted it was nothing to worry about. "House sounds," he said.

Now I will finally learn the truth. The light in the staircase leading to the attic blew out years ago, so I turn my phone flashlight on, holding it in one hand to illuminate my path to the top. The banister feels loose in my hand, but I grip it as I take the creaky stairs one at a time.

And then I reach the top.

I shine the flashlight beam on the lock on the doorknob. My hand is shaking as I fit the key into the lock. I swear I heard noises up there before, but now it is completely silent. Maybe Grant was telling the truth. Maybe this room is just a storage room, nothing more.

Or maybe there are dead bodies inside. Maybe Rebertha's corpse is rotting in this room.

Or maybe… there is somebody *alive* inside, waiting to pounce the second I unlock the door.

Slowly, I turn the key.

19

MY HEART IS DOING SPLIT LEAPS. I HEAR A CLICK—THE door is unlocked. I can now enter this forbidden attic room and learn the truth about what is inside. I push the door open...

It's a small space, about a quarter of the size of our bedroom, and very musty, like it hasn't been cleaned or dusted in years. It has only a single window, which is cracked open. There are some boxes pushed against the wall and a mannequin with a half-finished dress sewn to its body. And now, for the first time, I realize why I have heard noises coming from this attic room. I understand what the source of the mysterious sounds has been.

It's a Roomba. With a cat riding on it.

The cat lets out a surprised yowl when it sees me. It hops off the Roomba, which is still navigating its way between the boxes and sparse furniture. The cat rubs against my leg, looking at me expectantly, and when I don't offer it food, it gives me a dirty look and leaps out the cracked open window.

Okay, then.

The Roomba is now stuck in a corner of the room, making frustrated whirring noises. I shift my attention to the center of the room, where there is a rocking chair facing away from me, overlooking that one tiny window. The chair keeps rocking, back and forth, back and forth. It must be moving because of the breeze from the window. Unless…

Is somebody sitting in that chair?

I quickly walk around the side of the rocking chair, and when I see that it is empty, I let out a sigh of relief. There is nobody in the rocking chair. The room is entirely empty except for the Roomba, which is now banging against the wall repeatedly. No live people, no dead people—only the Roomba and I guess sometimes a cat who likes to ride it.

But there is something in the seat of the rocking chair—a small notebook. It's dusty, but not as much as the other items in the room. It looks like it might have been used within the last week or two. Frowning, I pick it up, and as I flip through the pages, thousands of lines of my husband's messy scrawl stare back at me.

Oh my God. It's a diary.

Grant kept a *diary*. I wouldn't have expected that of my husband—because really, who keeps a diary these days?—but that's clearly what this is. And now I can read it and potentially figure out the mystery of why I keep seeing him everywhere I go. I'm going to read two or three pages every day—maybe even four pages if I'm feeling ambitious. I am certain this diary will eventually reveal the answer, although at the pace I plan to read it, it will probably take me a few months to figure it out.

Gingerly, I sit down on one of the boxes and start to read.

20

Grant's Diary

THE GREAT DRAGON TORE THROUGH THE SKY, ITS majestic wings breaking through the mist of cumulus clouds, a symphony of power and grace. The awe-inspiring creature in the sky had deep-purple scales—each one a different brilliant shade—that covered its serpentine body, a long muscular tail ending in a sharp spade, a row of razor-sharp teeth, and eyes that burned with intelligence of the ages. To the dragon, I was but a tiny imperfection in the vast white landscape of snow that covered the earth.

"Someday," I said, "I will tame and ride that dragon."

A laugh echoed from behind me. I whipped my head around to find Zelvix Mistmael standing a few feet away, his muscular arms folded across the armor on his chest.

Zelvix smirked at me, his face chiseled in defined lines that oozed masculinity—a sculpted jawline that gave him an eternal air of determination—and waves of golden hair that caught the light with every movement. His perfect features were marred only by a jagged white scar on his forehead in the shape of a thundercloud, which he had earned in a battle in which our families had been pitted against each other. Now we were bitter enemies, and he had taken a solemn oath to someday kill me.

"You?" Zelvix snorted. "How could you tame that dragon? You are but a fae!"

21

Okay, it turns out it wasn't a diary.

Apparently, Grant decided to write a novel. And he decided that novel should be… a romantasy? Between a man named Zelvix Mistmael and a headstrong fairy named Furywa Wingrasmoril?

In any case, I don't think this notebook is going to hold the key to why I keep seeing Grant everywhere. And although I love a good romantasy, I'm really not enjoying his version very much. So I'm going to stop reading.

Oh well. So much for that.

I head back downstairs, and I don't bother to lock the attic behind me. I'm relieved there weren't any dead bodies up there but also a little disappointed. I hoped for an answer in that attic room, and I still don't have one. I still don't understand why my dead husband keeps appearing everywhere I go.

To distract myself, I grab all the casseroles from my refrigerator and load them into the trunk of my car.

There is no chance I will ever eat any of them, so the least I can do is bring them to Marnie. Well, actually, the least I can do is nothing. But I'll do one better and give her the casseroles.

As I'm slamming closed the trunk of my car, once again, I get that feeling like somebody is watching me. I turn around, and of course, nobody is there.

But then I hear a sound. A slight rustling in the hedges at the far corner of my lawn.

Grant used to be responsible for our lawn maintenance. Despite the fact that he worked long hours at the office, he took pride in making sure the grass on our lawn was green and healthy. The hedges are still perfectly trimmed, so much so that when I notice the irregularity in the hedge, I know with absolute certainty there is something or *someone* within.

I also know that if somebody is hiding in those hedges, there is no way out. A high picket fence surrounds my property. Whoever is hiding will have to come out in plain sight in order to exit my lawn. I have them cornered.

I pop the trunk back open. The inside is now loaded with eight casserole dishes, but there's also something else—a shovel I keep in the trunk at all times in case I need to dig my car out of the snow in an emergency situation.

I remove the shovel and stride toward the hedges with more confidence than I feel. My heart is doing backflips, but my hands are surprisingly steady. It takes me a few seconds to cross the lawn, and I come to a halt in front of the hedge. The rustling has quieted, but I can tell from the shape that there is somebody hiding inside. I'm sure of it.

"I know you're in there," I say. "And you're not getting away this time."

And then I lift the shovel over my head.

I am prepared to bring it down with all my might. But before I can, a man leaps out, his hands in the air. He has dirty-blond hair and blue eyes and perfect chiseled features.

My husband is standing before me. The one who died in a fiery car wreck only two weeks ago. And now here he is, still alive.

I stare at him, the blood rushing in my ears. "Grant?"

Those familiar eyes meet mine. "No," he says. "I'm not Grant."

As much as I would love to believe that my husband didn't somehow come back to life, there is nobody who can tell me the man standing in front of me isn't Grant Lockwood. I was married to him, after all. I know what he looks like. And I know this is Grant.

But the next words out of his mouth change everything.

"I'm Brant. Grant's identical twin."

22

"What?" I say. "You're *what?*"

The man who looks exactly like my husband, who claims his name is Brant, still has his hands in the air. I lower the shovel, and he drops his hands.

"You're Grant's identical twin?" I say with undisguised skepticism.

"That's right."

"But that makes no sense." I punctuate my statement by digging the spade of the shovel into the grass. "Grant was an only child."

"He lied to you. He wasn't an only child. He had a brother—me."

"Still," I say. "It just seems so ridiculously unlikely. I mean, identical twins are really rare. And honestly, this all just seems like a cheap and overly convenient explanation for me seeing my dead husband everywhere. It sort of makes me want to roll my eyes."

"Well, *sorry*," Brant says. "What explanation would

you prefer? That Grant came back from the dead? Or maybe you're imagining the whole thing? How about if you're actually in a psychiatric hospital, and this entire marriage was completely in your head? Would that be better?"

"No, that's much worse."

"Exactly." He reaches into the back pocket of his blue jeans and pulls out a worn leather wallet. He fumbles around inside the wallet and finally pulls out an old, creased photo. "This was me and Grant as kids."

I take the photograph from his hands. It's a picture of two identical towheaded boys of about five years old, wearing shorts and T-shirts, who bear a striking resemblance to both each other and the man standing before me. It looks like it's been in his wallet for a very long time.

"This could have been faked," I say.

He plucks the photo from my hand and gingerly places it within the folds of his wallet. "So you say. But look at me, Alice. Do you really need a photograph to prove to you that I am identical to your late husband?"

Admittedly, this man does look very much like Grant. There is only one noticeable difference.

Brant notices where I'm looking and touches the side of his face, just a bit in front of his right ear, which is marked by a tiny mole about two millimeters in diameter. "It's the only difference between the two of us."

As I stare at Brant, the puzzle pieces start to fall into place. I didn't understand how Grant could have been home for dinner with me almost every night yet also had an entirely different family whose house was filled with photographs of him as a loving father. But now it suddenly makes sense.

"Marnie is *your* wife," I whisper.

"Yes," he says.

"But I don't understand. Why did you tell her your name is Grant?"

He clenches his teeth. "You don't understand what it was like for me growing up. Grant was always the better twin. He was always the one who everyone loved, who got the better grades in school, and then he landed an amazing job where he made a ton of money. He even has the better name between the two of us. I mean —*Brant*? That's the name of the snooty rich kid in some teen movie."

I can't disagree with his last point.

"Anyway," he continues, "when I met Marnie, I thought she was the most amazing person ever. All I wanted was for her to like me. And that's why, when she asked me what my name was, I told her it was Grant. I figured eventually I would tell her the truth." He frowns. "I suppose I let it go on a little too long."

"You think?"

He drops his head. "I have made some mistakes in my life. I won't deny that."

"I don't understand, though. Why does Marnie think *you're* dead?"

He lets out a long tortuous sigh. "I loved Marnie—I really did. But things have changed over the years. We aren't right for each other anymore, but she can't seem to accept it, because we have so, so, *so* many children together. That's why, when I heard about my brother's fatal accident, I realized this was a chance for me to finally escape my terrible marriage."

I flash back to the living room of Marnie and Brant's home. I remember looking at the photographs on the walls. The two of them seemed so happy together. But I know from experience that the smiles in photographs can be an illusion.

"Was it all the children?" I ask him. "Is that what put the strain on your marriage?"

He shakes his head now. "No, the kids are great. I'm sorry about that part—I'll genuinely miss my kids."

"Did you disagree on the color of that dress?"

"What?"

"Nothing. Never mind." I frown up at him. "So, what was it?"

"It's…" He digs his heel into the soil of our yard. "It's a little painful to admit. I… I don't know you very well, and I don't want you to think less of me."

"I won't think less of you."

"Please. I don't want to say it…"

There's pain in his eyes, which reminds me of the pain I felt during my marriage. I don't know what he was going through, but I am starting to suspect it was just as bad as my own situation. Like me, he clearly needs somebody to talk to.

"Tell me. Please, Brant."

"She…" He squeezes his eyes shut. "She doesn't like Nickelback. And I…" His Adam's apple bobs. "I love them. There—I said it. Nickelback is my absolute favorite band of all time, and my own wife can't stand them."

"Brant…"

"You have no idea what it's been like." He wipes his eyes with the back of his hand. "We'll be in the minivan together, and 'How You Remind Me' will come on the radio, and she'll say to me, 'Shut that awful music off.' She says they… they're super fake, and their songs are made for… entirely commercial reasons." His voice trembles dangerously, threatening to break. "She says that… *they're not even a real band*. She says nobody really likes them, and there must be something wrong with me." He lets out a strangled cry. "And now you probably think there's something wrong with me too."

I blink, staring at him in disbelief. "Brant, I *love* Nickelback."

He gives me a wary look. "You can't possibly mean that. You're just messing with me."

"No, I do! I love Nickelback! They have such a good vibe, their lyrics are so profound, and their tunes are a perfect mix of pop and grunge. They're my favorite band."

A slow smile spreads across his lips. "I… I thought I was the only one."

"I thought *I* was the only one!"

Our eyes meet, and for a moment, I wonder what my life would have been like if I had ended up with a different brother. I don't know Brant well, but it suddenly feels like we connect on a level that Grant and I never did. After all, we have something in common that very few people in the world do.

"I'm sorry I was following you," Brant says softly. "I didn't mean to scare you. I just wanted to make sure you were okay after my brother died."

"I'm okay," I say. "Actually, I am more than okay. Grant was… He wasn't always good to me. As Chad Kroeger would say, living with him damn near killed me."

"Although I enjoyed the Nickelback quote, I'm really sorry to hear that." Brant reaches out to gently touch my shoulder. "Grant did have issues. We had a difficult childhood, to say the least."

"Really? He never told me that."

"Yes, it was awful." He winces at the memory. "It was all those identical-twin studies we did when we were younger."

"Identical twin studies?"

"Yes, they were endless," Brant groans. "We were constantly having our IQ tested. On one occasion, we were both given marshmallows and told that if we were able to keep from eating them for five minutes, we would get a second marshmallow. And once, they sent Grant into space, and when he came back, they tested our blood, saliva, and urine to compare them. He was only six at the time!"

That does sound rather unpleasant. Although it doesn't excuse what he did to me.

"Listen," I say, "you had better come inside the house. If you stand out on the lawn long enough, one of the neighbors is going to see you."

He raises an eyebrow. "You trust me enough to let me into your house?"

I hesitate for a split second, but then I bob my head. Even though I only met Brant today, I feel an inexplicable connection to him. I trust him. I don't think he would hurt me.

I hope I'm not making a terrible mistake.

23

BRANT LOOKS AROUND OUR HOUSE, ASTONISHED. HE admires our seventy-two-inch television, runs his fingers along our antique armoire, and then sinks into the cushions of our Italian leather sofa with a groan of ecstasy.

"Wow," he finally says. "My brother did really well for himself." But he is looking directly at me when he says those words.

I clear my throat. "Let me put on a little music."

I tell Alexa to play Nickelback radio. As the tune of "Rockstar" fills the room, a smile spreads across Brant's handsome features. I hover over the sofa, uncertain how to approach this fairly unique situation. I mean, this man is the identical twin of the husband I murdered, and I didn't know he existed until five minutes ago. This can't happen to people very often.

"Can I get you something?" I ask. "Some tea?"

"I hate tea."

I gasp. "Oh my God, I hate tea too! I just… I only offered it to you because I thought…"

"It's okay," Brant says. "I understand. It's the same nightmare that I have lived."

I sink onto the sofa beside him, clasping my hands in my lap. "I don't know why, but I feel this strange connection to you."

"Because I look like Grant."

"No," I say firmly. "It's more than that. I never felt this way about Grant. I loved him, of course, but…"

"No, I understand." He furrows his brow. "That's how I felt about Marnie. I loved her, but there was always something missing. But now that I've met you… It feels like we are two sides of the same coin."

I lean forward eagerly. "Tell me what else you hate."

"I hate so many things," he muses. "I don't know where to begin. I… I hate any book that won the Pulitzer Prize. I hate people who use Android phones. I hate dark chocolate. I hate tomatoes when they're raw, but I love them when they're cooked. I hate when a mystery book ends on a cliffhanger and you're forced to read the second one just to find out who did it. I hate pennies."

I get this dizzy, giddy feeling. I hate *all* the same things that Brant hates. Especially pennies. I don't understand why we even still have them. They got rid of the halfpenny *centuries* ago.

"Also," he adds, "I hate that the United States is the only country that hasn't switched to the metric system. It makes me so mad!"

"The metric system is clearly the best unit of measurement," I say. "It makes so much more sense for everything to rely on multiples of ten. Like, twelve inches in a foot? What is *that*? And it doesn't in any way relate to 5,280 feet in a mile, which isn't even a multiple of twelve! Our current system is basically a conglomeration of incoherent measurement systems."

"I feel the exact same way," he whispers.

I never dreamed I would find my other half, but everything Brant is saying resonates with me so deeply. I didn't have these feelings even when Grant and I were still happy together. He didn't even *care* about the metric system. Brant is so very different from my husband, even beyond the tiny mole near his right ear.

Yet my feelings are so inappropriate. I can't fall for Brant. What would people think? And what about Marnie and all their many, many children?

"Would you like to have dinner with me tonight?" I blurt out.

"Yes," he replies instantly.

For the first time in a very long time, I feel a surge of happiness. The two of us exchange dopey-eyed smiles, and I can tell he's looking forward to this as much as I am. I don't know if there's any chance for a future between me and Brant, but I at least want to get to know him better.

"I have a few things I need to take care of," he tells me. "How about if I pick up some dinner, and I'll meet you back here at eight o'clock?"

"Sure," I say. "Um, what are you thinking for dinner?"

"How about McDonald's?"

I gasp again. "You read my mind."

Grant only liked the fancy things in life. He would

never have gotten a meal from a fast-food restaurant. Any life I would have with Brant would be very different from the one I had with my husband. And that is not a bad thing.

I escort Brant to my front door. He smiles at me one last time, and even though he's identical in appearance to my husband, at that moment, he somehow seems handsomer than Grant used to be. He lingers at the door, not leaving my home just yet. He stands there, his gaze fixed on mine.

"Alice," he says.

"Brant," I say.

And then before I know what's even happening, he leans in and presses his lips against mine. He kisses me in a way that Grant had not kissed me for a very long time. He kisses me until my legs go weak, and he has to hold me to keep me from sinking to my knees. It reminds me of that first kiss with Grant outside the French restaurant, where all the molecules of my body were exploding at once. I missed that feeling.

When he finally pulls away, we are both gasping for air. "I'll see you at eight," he promises.

I watch Brant disappear down the walkway to my home. Presumably, he's going to drive away in that green sedan, the same one he was following me in earlier.

Brant was the one following me. He said he was doing it because he was looking out for me, but when I think about it now, that explanation doesn't quite gel. If he wanted to look out for me, why wouldn't he have simply come to my front door and introduced himself?

Yet my gut is telling me that I can trust Brant Lockwood.

Since I'm not going over to Marnie's house right now, I rescue the casseroles from my car and return them to my overstuffed fridge. The casseroles get me thinking about Poppy and how worried she's been about me the last couple of days, so I decide to head over to her house to spill the beans about what just happened. Poppy is my best friend, and she has a great way of looking at things. I'll tell her everything that Brant said to me—her reaction will tell me if she thinks I can trust him.

Poppy has been my next-door neighbor for the last five years. She lives in a colonial-style house just to the right of my property. Unlike my sprawling new home, hers is simple and rectangular and symmetric with a steep side-gable roof. Usually, she comes to my house rather than vice versa. As I am stepping through her walkway, which is slightly overgrown with weeds from her garden, it occurs to me that I have not been to her house in quite a while.

The front door of Poppy's home is right in the center of the property, with a number of small multi-paneled windows surrounding it. I press my finger against the doorbell, waiting for my friend to let me in.

It takes several seconds. Finally, I hear shuffling behind the door. But when it swings open, Poppy is not the one standing before me. It's an elderly woman with snow-white hair pulled into a bun behind her head. She is stooped over, with a cane in her gnarled hand.

She looks up at me with a questioning expression on her face. "Can I help you, dear?"

"Oh," I say. "I was just… Is Poppy home?"

"Poppy?"

"Poppy Durden," I say. "She lives here."

The elderly woman frowns up at me, and the next words out of her mouth chill me to the bone. "Nobody by that name lives here."

24

Nobody by that name lives here.

I gawk at the old woman. Clearly, she is just old and confused—perhaps an elderly aunt who is visiting Poppy for the week. "What are you talking about? Poppy has lived here for the last five years! She's my best friend!"

The woman twists the cane in her hand thoughtfully. "There was someone by that name who used to live here."

I don't know what she's talking about. Did Poppy suddenly decide to move without telling me? "Where did she go?"

"She died," the old woman tells me. "There was a terrible fire, and the woman named Poppy perished. But… that was thirty years ago."

My mouth is suddenly almost too dry to speak, and I have to force out my next words. "Are… are you sure?"

"Oh yes. I have lived here for years."

My entire universe has gone on tilt. I back away from the door, almost stumbling over the two steps to the front entrance. I don't know what's going on. All I know is I've got to get the hell out of here before my legs give out.

I hurry back to my own home as quickly as I can. I shut the door behind me, and I stand in the foyer, trying to catch my breath.

What just happened over there? Poppy has been my best friend ever since I moved here to live with Grant. And now this woman is telling me she doesn't live there —has *never* lived there. That the only Poppy who ever lived in that house was killed in a fire thirty years ago.

Did I imagine my best friend? Admittedly, it seems incredibly unlikely that I could somehow imagine an entire friendship with another human being who didn't even exist. It feels like if my brain were capable of doing something like that, I wouldn't be able to function in the real world. I mean, that is *really* out there.

Yet parts of it fit. Poppy has always been there for me when I needed her, always at *exactly* the right moment. She always told me the right things at the right time—always exactly what I needed to hear. Perhaps Poppy was my brain's way of coping with Grant tormenting me about that dress. Lord knows I needed it.

Man, I need to change all my emergency contacts to somebody who really exists.

Now that I realize that Poppy was just a figment of my imagination, I feel slightly lost. I had come to depend on her friendship so much in the last few years, but she wasn't even real. I am all alone now. Well, me and the baby growing inside me, but she won't be much comfort for a while.

But at least I have Brant. He is everything my husband was not, and in a few hours, we will share a delicious dinner together, possibly from the dollar menu. I can't wait to see him again. Everything is going to be okay.

25

At eight o'clock on the dot, my doorbell rings.

Brant is prompt—I appreciate that. Grant was so busy with work—it felt like he never got home for dinner on time. So I am grateful that his identical twin brother is more in line with my own sense of timeliness.

When I pull open the front door, Brant is standing before me in the same worn pair of blue jeans and gray T-shirt he was wearing earlier. Grant would never have dressed that way, but even so, Brant looks so incredibly handsome. And he looks achingly like my husband—well, aside from that tiny mole near his right ear.

He's clutching a brown paper bag with the McDonald's logo on it. And in his other hand, he is holding a gift-wrapped box.

"I got you a little present," he says. "I hope you don't mind."

He even figured out that I like presents. He really is very intuitive about me.

Brant drops the brown paper bag on my coffee table,

and the two of us sit on the sofa. The smell of fried oil fills the living room, and my stomach growls audibly.

He laughs. "Hungry?"

"Starving." I hold my breath, knowing that Brant is not aware of my secret. But if we are about to become friends—and possibly more—he deserves to know the truth. "I'm actually… I'm eating for two right now."

His eyes widen. "You're pregnant?"

I nod slowly, watching his reaction. "I only found out after Grant died. We were trying for a long time, but…"

How could I have gotten LED and IUD mixed up? Honestly, they should put some sort of warning on the box of LED lights: *These lights will not prevent pregnancy.*

But Brant doesn't seem upset. Just the opposite. "That's amazing, Alice!"

"It doesn't change things, does it?" I lick my lips. "I mean, the fact that I am pregnant with Grant's baby?"

"Grant and I share the same DNA," he reminds me. "So any baby of his is actually just as closely related to me as my own child."

"So… you don't mind?"

"Of course not! I love kids! I've always…" He stops talking midsentence and instead just smiles at me. "I think it's amazing. I really do."

"I'm so relieved." My shoulders relax, and I return his smile. "And I'm glad this child won't be raised by Grant. She will be raised by two parents who understand that the metric system is far superior to imperial units."

"That's right. Every morning, we will send her to school with two hundred fifty milliliters of milk." Brant tugs on the neck of his T-shirt and makes a face. "Alice, I hate to ask this, but would you mind very much if I changed into one of Grant's outfits? I've been wearing the same set of clothes for the last two weeks, and I'm dying to put on something fresh."

Grant was very protective of his clothing, but I suppose it doesn't matter now. After all, he's dead, so he won't mind. "Go for it."

"Thank you." He wags his finger. "Also, you have to promise me you won't open your present before I get back."

"I can wait." I dip my hand into the McDonald's bag. "As long as I don't have to wait for the french fries."

He laughs. "I would never be so cruel."

I duck into the kitchen to grab a glass of water to go with the food, because you definitely can't eat McDonald's french fries without water. I stuff a bunch of the fries into my mouth, savoring the way they melt on my tongue. There is nothing like the pure, unadulterated pleasure of eating greasy french fries.

"Okay!" a voice calls out from the second floor. "I'm back!"

I tilt my head to look up at the top of the stairwell. Brant is freshly dressed in one of Grant's Armani suits. I suck in a breath as I watch him descend the stairs. As devastatingly handsome as he looks, I wish he had put on something besides one of the suits. In jeans and a T-shirt, Brant resembled Grant very strongly, but now that he is wearing one of those suits, it almost feels like my dead husband has come back to life.

Brant cocks his head to the side. "Are you okay, Alice?"

"Yes," I sputter. "Of course. I just… In that suit, you look so much like…"

His brow crinkles. "Oh… is it making you uncomfortable? Would you like me to change?"

"No…" I manage a smile. I'm being silly. "That's okay. It's fine."

He comes around the side of the couch and sits beside me. He has a boyish smile on his face that reminds me of a child on Christmas Day. He picks up the gift-wrapped box and holds it out to me. "Now it's present time."

I beam at him, pushing aside any remaining anxiety about the suit he's wearing. "Thank you. You are so thoughtful, Brant."

I take the box from him. I shake it, hoping to hear candy rattling around inside. But no. It feels more like something soft. I'm so excited to find out what he got for me. I hope it's a new scarf. And not a warm scarf, but one of those useless silky ones.

I rip through the green wrapping paper and discover a square white box inside. I pause, smiling up at Brant. He winks at me.

"Go ahead," he says. "Open it."

Slowly, I lift the cover off the box. And when I see what's inside, my heart does a backspring followed by a split leap and then transitioning into a handspring on vault.

No. No, it couldn't be.

It's a blue-and-black dress.

26

"Do you like it, Alice?"

I raise my eyes to look up at the man sitting beside me in the Armani suit, with the dark-blond hair and blue eyes and the tiny mole near his right ear. He looks exactly the same as he did a moment earlier, but something in his voice has changed.

"What is this?" I whisper.

"It's a dress, silly," he says. "And I got it in your favorite colors. Blue and black." He cocks his head to the side. "You do like blue and black, don't you, Alice? Or would you have preferred something in white and gold?"

Fear grips my chest like a vise. "Who are you?"

"Or perhaps yellow and purple, if we're talking about ridiculous combinations," he goes on. "Or why not green and light green? Anything goes!"

"Grant?" I manage.

He arches one of his light-brown eyebrows. "How

could I be Grant? Grant is dead, isn't he? You killed him, didn't you?"

I let out an anguished cry, cowering on the sofa. "What's going on? What are you talking about, Brant?"

The man sitting beside me licks the tip of his index finger. Then he rubs against the side of his face until that tiny mole vanishes. Now that he is wearing that expensive suit, with the telltale mole apparently gone, there is no longer any doubt in my mind.

The man in front of me is Grant Lockwood.

"My twin brother was a good-for-nothing leech," he spits. "Always has been, always will be. He came to me a few weeks ago, trying to get me to give him some money for his ridiculously large family. If you can't support eight children, then don't have eight children! What a loser."

I don't know what to say. The words have flown out of my head, and all that remains is paralyzing fear.

"So I said to Brant that I couldn't give him any money," he continues, "but I told him I would give him my Mercedes. It was worth a lot of money, I told him, and he knew he could sell it. He was thrilled. Of course, I had already seen you messing around under my car. I knew the brakes would fail." A smile touches his lips. "After years of being a thorn in my side, my brother finally went down in a blaze of glory."

I scramble off the sofa, even though I'm not sure my legs will support me. I can't believe what I'm hearing. The man that I identified in the morgue was *Brant*, not Grant. I had noticed he was wearing different clothing from what Grant usually wears, but his shirt and pants were covered in blood, so I hadn't put much thought into it at the time.

"Did you really think you could get rid of me, Alice?" He grabs the blue-and-black dress that I left behind in the box. "Did you really think you could kill me and get away with it?"

Yes. Obviously, I did. But I can only mutely shake my head.

"Well, you were wrong." He rises to his feet and starts moving toward me. I take a step back, wondering if I could make a run for it. "Now, I want you to put on this dress."

"No," I squeak out. "I won't do it."

"You will do it!" he snaps. "And now that you're having my child, there are going to be some changes around here. First of all, I'm going to order you this dress in maternity sizes. Perhaps a pair of matching pants with an adjustable waistband."

"No!" I cry. "I won't wear it!"

"You will, though." He continues to move toward me as I back away. "You will do whatever I tell you to do."

"And if I don't?"

"I'm going to tell the police that you're the one responsible for my brother's accident. You'll go to jail for the rest of your life." He winks at me. "I already tipped off Detective Mancini."

Grant was the one who tipped off Mancini that the brakes in the car had been cut. I should have guessed.

He tilts his head thoughtfully. "Or perhaps I'll do the kinder thing and end your pathetic little life."

"No…" I take another step back and stumble against the wall. There is nowhere else to go. He has quite literally backed me into a corner. "You wouldn't do that. You wouldn't really kill someone."

"Maybe I would…" He holds each end of the blue-and-black dress in his fists so that the fabric forms the shape of a rope. "After all, I did it once. Nobody ever suspected that Rebertha's drowning at sea wasn't just a tragic accident."

I gasp. Grant killed his first wife too? I am stunned. When he told me about how they sailed out to the middle of the sea on his private yacht on the night of their third wedding anniversary and she slipped and fell off the deck with no witnesses, leaving him her vast fortune, it sounded so innocent.

"I can go to Marnie," he continues, "and tell her the real Grant is dead, and I can take over my brother's life. And with you out of the picture, Brant will be the next of kin and inherit all my money." He smiles proudly. "We will never have to listen to Nickelback again."

Tears well in my eyes, threatening to spill over. "You're a monster."

His eyes twinkle under the skylights. "Am I?"

"You're going to go to hell…"

He grins at me. "I'll see you there, then, won't I?"

I can't stop him. He's coming toward me with the blue-and-black dress fashioned into a noose. I imagine him wrapping it around my neck, squeezing and squeezing…

"Just think, Alice," he says. "Soon your face will be

blue. And when they put you in the ground, it will turn black."

I squirm against the wall, wondering if I can make a run for it, but I don't think I can. Grant is too close, and if I make any sudden moves, he will pounce. He's been planning this moment from the day we saw that striped dress on his computer screen. Soon, it will all be over. And nobody will ever suspect that Grant killed me, because as far as anyone knows, he is dead.

I place a hand on my belly. *I'm so sorry, little baby. I'm sorry I couldn't save you from this monster.*

Grant reaches out with the fabric of the dress taut between his fists, moving toward my neck, but before he can get there, a loud thump echoes through the room. And just like that, Grant goes limp and drops to the ground, unconscious.

I look up, confused. And when I see who is standing in front of me, my mouth drops open.

It's Poppy. And she's holding a shovel.

27

WHAT?

I am so confused. I went to Poppy's house earlier today, and I discovered that she doesn't exist, yet she somehow just saved my life. How is that possible?

"I was just about to knock on the front door, but then I heard shouting coming from inside," she tells me, brushing aside a strand of hair that has come loose from her messy bun. "So I grabbed a shovel that I found in your front yard and came in through the back." She looks down at Grant, lying unconscious on the floor. "Good thing I did."

I look from the shovel in Poppy's hands to my unconscious husband. "But... how did you do that?"

Poppy rests the shovel against the wall. "Do what?"

"How did you hit him on the head when I was standing over here?"

"Um, I just took the shovel and swung it as hard as I could. He went down pretty easily!"

"But…" I scrutinize the woman I thought was my best friend, from her yoga pants to her baggy T-shirt. She looks surprisingly real for a person I am hallucinating. I'm sort of impressed with my brain right now. "But you're not real. You're all in my head."

"I'm *what*?"

"You're a figment of my imagination," I clarify. "I fabricated you as a way to deal with my husband and his obsession."

"Um, excuse me?" She plants a hand on her hip. "I just saved your life by hitting your homicidal husband on the head with a shovel, and now you're repaying me by telling me that I'm not real?"

"But you're not," I insist.

"So how did I hit Grant on the head with a shovel?"

I drop my gaze to my own palms. "I must've hit him on the head with that shovel. Somehow."

Poppy rolls her eyes. "Okay, and what about those five casseroles I brought you?"

"I must have made them myself."

"How about the times I drove you to the mall, and we went shopping together?"

"I must've been driving."

"What about when I made that huge charcuterie platter for book club, with all those little prosciutto roses I spent hours shaping?"

"I guess *I* made the charcuterie tray and shaped all those roses myself." Poppy gives me a look, and I shrug helplessly. "I'm sorry. Believe me, I genuinely wish you were real. But I went over to your house a few hours ago, and…" I gesture out the window at the colonial-style house where the old woman had turned me away. "There was somebody else living there. She told me that there had been a Poppy living there many years ago, but she died in a fire."

Poppy gawks at me. "Alice, seriously? You know I live in the house on the *left*, don't you? That's Mrs. Hubbard on the right, and she is completely confused half the time."

"What?"

"Oh my God." She blows out a breath between her teeth. "This is why it's annoying that I am always the one coming over to your house. Maybe if you came over to *my* place a little more often, you would know where I freaking live, Alice."

"Oh." Now that she mentioned it, I do remember that Poppy's house is the yellow one on the left. Oops, my mistake. "Sorry about that."

Grant starts to stir on the carpet below us. He mumbles something, and his eyes crack open. He looks like he's about to try to get up again, but honestly, I'm just ready to be done with this. I glance over at Poppy, and then without another word, I pick up the shovel that is still leaning against the wall. And I bring it down on Grant's scalp. Then I do it again.

And again.

And again.

Poppy watches the whole thing, but she doesn't stop me. When I'm done, there's blood all over the carpet and the shovel. But Grant isn't moving anymore.

"He's dead." I let the shovel drop out of my hand and clatter to the floor. "The nightmare is finally over."

"Not yet."

I raise my eyes. "What do you mean?"

"We still have to bury the body."

28

POPPY AND I SPEND THE NEXT TWO HOURS BURYING MY husband in my backyard.

All I have to say is that I am super sure she is not imaginary, because there is no way I could have done it on my own. I find an extra shovel in the garage, and we dig a hole large enough to throw Grant's body inside. We dig through the soil to a depth of about three feet, hoping it's enough to keep the animals away.

And nobody will be looking for Grant, since everybody already thinks he is dead. Although I still have to deal with Detective Mancini.

Together, we pick him up and throw him into the shallow grave. He's still wearing his fancy suit, and even though all the muscles of his body have relaxed in death, he is still clutching that blue-and-black dress in his right hand.

"You will never, ever let it go, will you?" I murmur.

He doesn't answer.

We don't stop to say a few words in his honor. We

quickly shovel the dirt back into the grave, covering my husband's body. Only when we have scooped the last of the dirt back into the hole and smoothed over his grave does Poppy lay a hand on my shoulder.

"Alice," she says, "you're holding your breath."

"I am?"

"Yes, you are."

"Oh my gosh!" I clasp a hand to my chest. "I hadn't even realized it! Thanks for letting me know."

I let out the breath. It's finally over. Thank God.

Poppy and I are both caked in dirt and blood. She brushes off her hands on her yoga pants and then examines them critically. "Do you mind if I take a shower before I go home? I'd rather my husband didn't see me walking in with my hands covered in blood."

"Sure," I say. "And I've got a clean dress you can put on when you're done."

I'm going to give Poppy the blue-and-black dress that I've been keeping in my closet as a reminder of what Grant did to me in case I ever decided it was a mistake to get rid of him. After killing my husband twice, I don't need that reminder anymore.

We climb the stairs to the bedroom, and Poppy showers in my master bathroom. My hands are covered in blisters from the shovel, my fingernails caked with dirt. I'm going to take a long, hot shower after Poppy is done, but no amount of hot water will get rid of the damage.

On top of the dresser are the pair of jeans and the T-shirt that Grant was wearing when he first walked in. I'll have to burn them. I pick up the jeans, and Grant's wallet falls out of the back pocket, dropping to the floor. I look at it for a second, debating whether I should get rid of it. But then I shove it into the top drawer of my dresser. Something tells me there's a chance I might need it someday.

The running water in the shower sputters to a halt. After a few moments of rustling inside the bathroom, the door bursts open so quickly that it slams into the wall. Poppy has a towel wrapped around her chest, her damp hair dripping onto the bedroom carpet, and she looks furious.

"Why didn't you tell me about this, Alice?" she cries as she shakes something in my face.

I frown at her. "What are you talking about?"

Then I realize what she has in her hand. It's the pregnancy test that I threw in the trash. "How come you didn't tell me?"

"I did tell you!" I might be forgetting things, but I remember our conversation. "I told you I was pregnant."

"Pregnant?" She looks down at the test in her hand and then back at my face. "Alice, this is a Covid test."

"What?" I gasp. "How could that be?"

"It literally says *Covid-19 Ag* right on the test!"

"It does?" Wow, maybe it's time for reading glasses.

Poppy lets out a huff. "You didn't really think this was a pregnancy test, did you?"

"Well…" I chew on my lower lip. "I was in a hurry, and I wasn't thinking straight. I just grabbed one of the tests that showed the two blue lines on the box. I *did* think it was a little strange that I had to swab my nose to check for pregnancy."

Huh. It looks like those LED lights worked after all. I can't believe I'm not really pregnant. I wonder why I was so nauseous—I guess it was the tea.

Poppy grits her teeth. "Oh my God, I cannot *believe* you have Covid."

"Now that you mention it, I did have a little bit of a runny nose and sore throat…"

"Ugh, and I have a wedding to go to in a few days. This is just great. The perfect end to this day, seriously."

"Sorry." I smooth out the rumpled blue-and-black dress from my closet. "I honestly didn't know."

Poppy plops down on my bed in frustration. "Okay, well, thanks for giving me Covid, Alice."

A news alert goes off on my phone. I pick it up, and a news report flashes on the screen about a convenience-store robbery that took place downtown. One police officer was killed during the robbery. Detective Mancini.

I had been worried about Mancini investigating Grant's accident. He seemed determined to get to the truth, and I was terrified that he would never stop. But apparently, he will no longer be investigating. Because he's now dead.

And he had only one week left until retirement.

Poppy raises her eyebrows, but I just shake my head. She doesn't need to know about the investigation. She's already helped me enough, and I might have given her Covid. I don't need to add to her stress. I hope it really is completely and truly over.

"Anyway," Poppy says, "let me go get dressed. You said you had something for me to wear?"

I hold out the hanger with the dress hanging off of it. The annoyance evaporates from Poppy's face as she looks at the dress, and she smiles up at me.

"Thank you, Alice," she says. "I love white and gold."

EPILOGUE

I SLEEP LIKE THE DEAD AFTER BURYING MY HUSBAND IN the backyard. I thought I would be plagued by restless dreams of zombie husbands scraping their way through the dirt and shuffling into my bedroom, hungry for brains. I thought I would be waking up in a cold sweat, a scream on my lips. But instead, I get the best night of sleep I have had in years—not one zombie-husband dream. I don't wake up even once, and when my eyes finally crack open, the sun is already high in the sky.

For the first time in a long time, I am truly free. And it feels fantastic.

I stretch in bed, raising my arms high over my head and reaching with my toes toward the foot of the bed. I let out a long, luxurious yawn that lasts several seconds. I plan to enjoy this day as much as I possibly can. On my own.

One thing I will do today is write a great big check for Marnie, even though Grant was never her husband. Now that I don't have a baby on the way, I can afford to be generous. I feel responsible for her well-being, considering that I, you know, accidentally murdered her husband.

I roll out of bed, intending to take a long, hot shower, but then I realize the shower is already running. The bathroom door is closed, and the distinctive sound of droplets of water hitting the porcelain of the tub floats into the bedroom.

What's going on? Why is the shower on?

I suppose I could have left it on last night. But no, that doesn't make sense. If I left the shower on, I would have noticed it when I went to sleep. No, it's clear that someone entered our bathroom and turned on the shower and *is in there right now*.

My heart is doing one-hundred-meter dashes as I slide out of bed in my blue silk nightgown. I pad across the bedroom in the direction of the master bathroom. I push open the door with a trembling hand, and sure enough, the shower is running. The entire bathroom is fogged up with steam, but I can make out the silhouette of a man behind the glass doors.

Almost like I'm in a trance, I move forward. In the back of my head, it occurs to me that I could be in danger, but I can't make myself stop. When I reach the shower, my hand shoots out and opens the glass doors to reveal the naked man inside. My breath catches at the sight of the man standing in my shower, his bare skin pink from the steaming-hot water, his blond hair plastered to his scalp as he swivels his head to offer me a smile.

"Good morning," says a man who looks exactly like my husband.

No. *No.*

I rub my eyes, wondering if I'm imagining the man in our shower. But even after shutting my eyes for the count of three and then reopening them, he is still there. His foggy silhouette is massaging shampoo into his hair. He is most definitely real.

I shut the door to the shower and stumble out of the bathroom, my head spinning. How could this be? It's impossible. I killed my husband and buried him—twice. Well, the first time I killed his brother, but the second time it was most definitely him. Yet here he is, showering in our bathroom like nothing ever happened.

It was all a dream.

No, wait. It can't have been a dream because my hands are covered in calluses from the shovel last night, and there is still some dirt ground into my fingernails. I definitely buried somebody last night. I didn't dream it.

So what is going on here?

The alarm goes off on my phone, practically jolting me out of my skin. The ringtone is one of my favorite Nickelback songs, "Photograph." My body stands rigid as the insightful lyrics about looking at photographs wash over me.

Wait. That's *it.*

My head is buzzing as I head straight for the dresser and yank open the top drawer where I shoved Grant's wallet last night. I flip it open and finger through the photographs. It takes me a few seconds to find the one

I'm looking for—the photograph of Grant and his identical twin brother.

I pull out the old, creased photo. I stare at the identical towheaded boys in the picture. When Grant showed me this photo, I noticed something about it, but I couldn't quite put my finger on it. It didn't hit me until this second what was wrong with this photo.

Gently, I reach behind the photo and unfold the left corner.

Now I can see the photograph in its entirety. And I finally realize what I am looking at. I had thought it was a photo of two brothers playing together. But instead of Grant and Brant alone, the full image reveals there are actually *three* little boys.

Oh my God.

Identical triplets.

THE END

ACKNOWLEDGMENTS

Okay, my cat is looking at me like she wants to write the acknowledgments too, so I better do this quickly.

I want to thank all the many beta readers I had on this project. My mother, who couldn't stop laughing at the twin studies. My father, who came up with the idea for Willie. Also thanks to Pam, Nelle, Jenna, Kate, Emily, Rebecca, Maura, Beth, and Val for all the feedback. Thank you to Red Adept Editing for… editing.

Thank you to all the many Facebook thriller groups for pointing out every single thriller cliche that I was able to utilize in this book. Trust me when I say that those posts have brought a smile to my lips, even if it didn't touch my eyes.

Of course, the biggest thanks of all goes to Nickelback, my second most played band on Spotify in 2022. Your rock/pop hits have been an enjoyable soundtrack during hundreds of sprints on the treadmill, and that's how you remind me how awesome you are. Also, my husband loves you too.

AFTERWORD

Did you enjoy reading *The Widow's Husband's Secret Lie?*

If so, please consider leaving a review on Amazon! Also, check out my website, where you can sign up for my newsletter and get updates on my books:

http://www.freidamcfadden.com/

You can also sign up for my newsletter directly. And to get updates about new releases, please <u>follow me on Amazon</u>! You can also <u>follow me on Bookbub</u>! Or join my super cool and fun reader group, <u>Freida McFans</u>!

Usually at this point, I put a little excerpt from my next book. But this time, I'm going to do something a bit different. I've written a short story inspired by my next book, *The Boyfriend*. Keep reading to check it out…

BAD DATE SOS!!!

SOS!!!!!

What's wrong?

I'm on the worst date ever! Please help!

You have said that so many times, the words have lost all meaning.

I mean it this time. SOS! 911! Worst. Date. Ever.

Help me!

Which guy was it?

It was that guy Edgar. Age 32, 5'10, never married.

Not ringing a bell.

The one who didn't like pizza.

Oh, right! Who doesn't like pizza?

Clearly only a psychopath, judging by my date tonight.

OK, so what happened that was so awful?

Syd?

Sydney?

Sorry, got pulled away for a moment.

Anyway, Edgar and I were supposed to meet at that bar and grill on 18th street for dinner but I got there a few minutes early. I ordered a beer, thinking it would come just as he arrived, but no. I had time to finish the whole thing and he still hadn't come.

So he no-showed?

I wish. I had paid for the beer and I was about to leave when he finally arrived, twenty minutes late.

OK, that's pretty bad.

And get this, he's holding this duffel bag. This huge duffel bag that's as big as I am. And I'm like, did you just get back from a trip? And he's like, no.

Then he stuffs it under the table without answering and asks if I know where the bathroom is so he can wash his hands.

What's wrong with that? I like when guys wash their hands before a meal.

Yeah, me too. But then I look down at his hands and they're absolutely covered in... I don't know what. Something dark red.

Red???

Exactly.

Did you ask him what it was?

He said cranberry juice.

Why would he have cranberry juice all over his hands?

I DON'T KNOW!!!

Why didn't you just slip out while he was in the bathroom?

I would have, except he told me that I needed to watch the duffel bag. And I was scared to leave it. I mean, it was REALLY big. What if there was something valuable in it? So I stayed.

Except then he comes back and I notice that red stuff is on his shirt collar too. And one of his sleeves. It's sort of freaking me out, but he keeps insisting it's cranberry juice.

OMG that sounds terrible.

Syd?

Sydney?

SYDNEY???

Sorry sorry, I'm here.

But this is getting scary, Gretchen.

When I saw all those red stains, I thought about leaving, but you know I hate to do that, and he was pretty cute, so I stuck around. We even ordered some fries to share.

Not so bad.

But then I hear this strange sound coming from under the table. It almost sounds like a woman's voice. And I'm like, WTF is that??

A woman's VOICE????

I'm contorting myself to look down under the table, and I realize that the sound is coming from INSIDE THE DUFFEL BAG.

Noooo....

So I'm like, Edgar, what's in the bag? And he's like, oh, just some stuff. And he doesn't want to tell me.

But then I hear it again—the woman's voice. And I was pretty sure the bag was moving.

You should have opened it!

Are you out of your everloving mind??? I wasn't opening that bag!

I would have opened it.

You are so full of it. You would not.

You don't know that.

Whatever, you're afraid to even open your heating bill.

That's completely different.

ANYWAY

So while we're sitting there, we hear this police siren from outside and Edgar looks totally freaked out. He ducks down, like he doesn't want anyone to see him.

Also, that's when I notice he's got a long scratch on his jaw, like he was in some kind of scuffle. So at that point, I'm like, I'm out of here, seriously.

So... you left?

Well, no. Because the French fries came with this zesty dipping sauce, and I felt bad leaving right when the food arrived.

Plus, I was very hungry.

So you risked your life for fries.

I wasn't risking my life! We were in a public place.

But then when we were eating the fries, something terrible happened...

What? Did he double dip?

No, he took each French fry, opened it up, and then ate just the INSIDE of the fry. He was eating the fries like they were baked potatoes!

What a maniac.

I know! And THEN he double dipped. He double dipped his massacred French fry.

That's horrific.

After watching him do that like four or five times, I was just done. I was ready to take off. But then there were more sirens outside and he seemed completely panicked.

Finally, he's like, can you watch my bag while I run and get something from my car? And apparently, his car is right outside the door.

Where on earth did he park? There's never street parking there.

He parked in a handicapped spot.

What??

He said he saved the placard from when his grandma was still alive.

OMG, what an asshole.

I know, right?

So I figure I'll just wait for him to get whatever it is from his car, then we'll call it a night. He runs out to the car, and I'm hoping he'll take that duffel bag with him but he DOESN'T.

I can see the car from my seat, and he's doing SOMETHING in the car, and all the while, the sounds from under the table are getting louder. It DEFINITELY sounds like a woman's voice. A woman's voice saying, WHY? I was pretty sure.

Why what?

Exactly. Why WHAT? And then

Sydney?

Sydney??

SYDNEY, ARE YOU OK???

Sorry, ugh.

You are freaking me out!

It's OK, I'm hanging in there.

Anyway, he was doing something in the car for like forever. FINALLY, he comes back out and you won't believe what he's got with him.

A severed head?

No.

A machete?

Worse!

He's got a BABY.

A baby???

Yes! He's got this baby that's like six months old and it's in a carseat, which has apparently been in his car the whole time.

I guess that's why he was freaked out that the police were going to see the baby all alone in there while his dad was on a date.

Whoa.

And get this, the baby is holding a bottle with something red in it and he's sucking it down, but also spilling it everywhere. I guess that was the cranberry juice that got all over everything.

Are babies allowed to drink cranberry juice?

How should I know??

I don't think they are.

I don't think that baby got the memo.

Anyway, Edgar starts going on and on about his ex, and how she doesn't let him spend enough time with the baby, so that's why when she gave him some time with the baby, he couldn't say no and had to bring him on our date.

Wow, what a great dad.

And the best part is that the baby STINKS. Like he needs a diaper change.

So I gently point it out, and he's like, oh, I'm bad at that, could you do it?

You didn't do it, did you???

Well, I didn't WANT to, but I also felt bad for the baby.

You were just enabling that guy's bad behavior!

Oh, trust me, he was NOT changing that diaper. And I'm sure the baby didn't like sitting in its own filth and cranberry juice.

So I'm like, OK fine, where are the diapers? I figure I'll change the baby, then go.

You're WAY too nice.

So he's like, the diapers are in the duffel bag. Then he grabs it from under the table and unzips it. And there's practically a baby STORE in that bag. He's got diapers, pacifiers, rattles, and even this horrible vibrating box that has a woman's voice basically shouting the alphabet.

The alphabet?

I guess it was a learning toy.

Anyway, she wasn't saying WHY, she was saying Y.

Well, at least it wasn't a woman imprisoned in the bag.

Trust me, that would have been better. This bag was GROSS.

And worst of all, the one thing he didn't have was baby wipes. So he's like, let me go out to the car and get some wipes.

Meanwhile, I move to sit next to the baby strapped into his carseat, and I'm helping the baby hold the bottle filled cranberry juice so it doesn't spill, but the cap must be defective because it gets all over my hands too.

I hope you gave him an earful when he came back.

Well, that's the thing. He left the bar over twenty minutes ago and hasn't come back.

And now it looks like his car is gone.

WHAT???

I know! AND I DON'T EVEN HAVE BABY WIPES.

I can't believe he left his baby with you.

Maybe he had another date and I'm the babysitter. And also

Wait, hang on, the baby spit up and I need to wipe it up.

Sorry I have to keep dealing with this.

OMG.

OK, I'm back.

You have to call the police.

Ugh, no. Maybe he'll come back? And the baby is pretty cute. I just wish I could turn off that stupid toy. It's been through the entire alphabet EIGHTEEN times.

It doesn't have an off switch. I don't even know where the batteries are. It doesn't seem to HAVE batteries in it.

I think it might be possessed.

Syd, he abandoned his child. You have to call the police.

Yeah, you're right. OK, I'm going to

Syd?

Wait, I see his ex walking into the bar!

How do you know it's her?

He showed me a picture of her.

Of course he did.

That's definitely her!

OK, looks like I'm off the hook! TTYL!

Message left two hours later:

Gretchen, I need your help!

I was taken to jail on kidnapping charges and I need help finding a lawyer.

SOS!!!!

If you enjoyed this little short story, for more creepy dating fun, please grab a copy of The Boyfriend!

ALSO BY FREIDA MCFADDEN

The Boyfriend

The Teacher

The Coworker

Ward D

Never Lie

The Inmate

The Housemaid is Watching

The Housemaid's Secret

The Housemaid

Do You Remember?

Do Not Disturb

The Locked Door

Want to Know a Secret?

One by One

The Wife Upstairs

The Perfect Son

The Ex

The Surrogate Mother

Brain Damage

Baby City

Dead Med

The Devil Wears Scrubs

The Devil You Know

ABOUT THE AUTHOR

Freida McFadden is a *#1 New York Times*, Amazon Charts, *Wall Street Journal*, *Washington Post*, *USA Today*, *Publishers Weekly*, and OMG this list just goes on forever, doesn't it? Enough. Freida writes books, okay?

Freida is also a part-time practicing physician, but she's not a surgeon and doesn't know how that rumor got started. Freida lives with her family and black cat in a centuries-old three-story home overlooking the ocean where nobody can hear you if you scream, trust me.

Printed in Great Britain
by Amazon